A Tale of
Three Cities

By Teresa Meyerhoeffer Christensen

Cover created by Halle Brianne Huber

ISBN-13: 978-1732880252

ISBN-10: 1732880255

Bridge2WorldsBooks
5942 Harvest Point Circle
Mountain Green, Utah 84050

www.TeresaMeyerhoefferChristensen.com

Dedicated to all ten cities
that added upon whom I have become…

Moscow, Buhl, Twin Falls, Boise (Idaho)
Ontario, Corvallis, Bend, Hood River (Oregon)
North Salt Lake and Mountain Green (Utah)

Hopefully, I left something of good
behind in your boundaries as well.

Other books by this author:

Love More Judge Less (non-fiction)

The Least of 3's

DROUGHT

Hijacking Happiness (non-fiction)

There is Love

Not Really Homeless

Seth Row

Angels Unshelved

Scenic Solar Loop Traveler's Brochure:

Welcome to the Scenic Solar Loop! This trip will take travelers from elevations just above sea level to soaring heights reaching above 7000 feet (2133 meters) while passing many geographic wonders including...Meteor Mountain, Cosmos Lake, Milky Way Falls, Asteroid River, and more. Tourists will weave through marshlands and moors experiencing various terrains, unique forms of vegetation, and many fresh bodies of water on the drive, eventually summiting rocky forested peaks where pull-outs offer views of the vast vistas below. Three cities dot the landscape along the way to offer refreshments and cultural side opportunities should any be desired. Please take time to visit Starville, Moonburg, or Sunlight City on the drive if so inclined. Plan on three hours to complete this tour without stops, however, interested travelers should reserve at least one whole day to fully appreciate what nature has to offer in this spectacular area.

CITY ONE

Sunlight City

Residing on top of a mountain has its advantages. The morning sun cresting the tall peaks creates an alpenglow that warms me from one end to the other whatever the season. Light permeates everything at this elevation, and it seems as if I touch the sky as the clouds roll by overhead. The heavenly expanse above is endless.

My surroundings are draped with dense forest, but a broad level clearing was prepared to lay the infrastructure and foundations where I reside. Wildflowers grow without assistance in my soil, even so, other vegetation has been planted and grows nicely to compliment what I freely offer. If I could pick any place to dwell, it would probably be right here or in a place very similar. Beauty abounds all around me and makes me feel alive.

I am approaching one hundred years old next year. I wonder if my associates will throw me a party for all that I have been to them. I'm still in pretty good shape, but my size varies and grows as does the population with time and seasons. Fewer bodies live here in the winter and things feel thinner. The altitude causes much cooler weather, and the vaster snowfall draws a different breed. I cannot leave of course, but I wouldn't want to. Every season has something grand to offer.

The air up here is void of contaminants and so fresh. Smells could be bottled as perfume. And the swift-flowing water that crosses my mid-section is pure and as crystalline clear as glass. The water has been bottled so it is just a matter of time before they figure out how to capture the scents of the air in a container as well.

Many species of life share my space, from tiny insects too small to be easily seen to the large black bears that hibernate in the hollows of my trees. Grubs, maggots, and snakes crawl across my decomposing leaf-strewn surfaces. Squirrels, rabbits, fox, wildcats, deer, and bear roam upon my forest floor and birds of several varieties fly overhead. I have become a full-on wildlife refuge. This function is one of my dearest destinies.

The people living amid and across me seem to be happy, clean, and good, not fancy, or ostentatious. Their clothes are practical and well-made, brightly colored with earth hues like those of their surroundings. My inhabitants come across sincere without a facade. A community of humans who are literally above all the pettiness of the world. Perhaps these people are pleased to merely be alive and don't require all of the extras that are often deemed to be needed these days. I hesitate to admit that I have my preferred favorites. Some local dwellers treat me better than others and a few even bring me joy. Aiden Birdwhistle has always been a bright spot among the men who reside here ever since he was a boy. The young man goes out of his way to do what he can to keep my boundaries infused with clean energy and light. His positive spirit permeates my very essence as does that of a few others that dwell here. I embrace all light-imbuing entities.

Industries have found a home and grown within my parameter. Solar energy has drawn those who seek work up here to perfect and install it. The actual manufacturing is done in one of the cities lower in geography thank goodness. A sister city can deal with the grime and pollution that mass production can cause. There is also a bottled spring water company called Solar-Sparkled Water. The water does sparkle as it flows through the stream, but I am not sure if it still does when captured in a bottle. Most things that are imprisoned lose some of their absorbed and reflected light. They draw the sparkling water from the stream belt that runs across my middle strip, but the water is always replenished from annual run-off and seasonal rains, so it never runs dry. My sacrifice of water is somewhat similar to the donating of blood that humans do to help one another survive.

The most entertaining operation in our midst is a contraption they call a 'ski lift' that hauls humans up the hill with slender sleds also called skis strapped upon each foot or a larger board that both feet can fit into. After debarking the chairlift at the top, they swish and slide all the way back down to the bottom of the slope and do it over and over again until exhausted. The maneuver sort of tickles from my end.

Sometimes I wonder how old I will live to be. Or if anyone who contributes something meaningful for the world as a whole will emerge from my boundaries. At times, I wish I could visit my sisters and see how they are doing but realize we each have our own destinies to fulfill right where we are. Most other living creatures who cross my path don't understand that I have feelings too. We are all part of a greater consciousness here on earth. Each of us trying to do and give our best within the boundaries which we are given.

Chapter 1

Our Sun is all of the colors mixed together which appears white to the human eye. The Sun is also almost a perfect sphere. There is a ten-kilometer difference between the Sun's polar and equatorial diameters. This means it is the closest thing to a perfect sphere that has been observed in nature.

Aiden

On some level, Aiden Birdwhistle knew that he was driving too fast and slightly out of control along the two-lane highway but even if his truck had suddenly elevated off the asphalt and taken off in flight he probably would not have noticed. His mind was rotating even faster than the four all-season radial tires on his vehicle. The image of the Mayor's dead body bleeding out on the carpeted office floor right in front of him was all that he could think about. The visual haunted and consumed his every thought.

Why hadn't he stayed and called the police or at least 911? Why did he just flee the scene? That would not look good. At least he had checked for a pulse but finding no comforting heartbeat present he had panicked. The man was already gone. Who else knew that he had been there? The Mayor's secretary must have seen his name on the schedule. There were definitely issues between Mayor Dankworth and the Birdwhistle family but that was just business. Aiden would never have killed the guy. Would the police think he had enough motive to do something that awful?

Aiden took the next corner several miles per hour over the posted speed limit and almost veered off of the pavement correcting just in time to prevent the inertia from carrying him into a ditch. This morning before the sun came up over the mountain, he had driven the two hours to Starville for a business meeting with the Mayor. His family owned a small solar panel company called *Sunbeams in a Box*. They sold and installed the panels anywhere along the solar loop, but their actual product was manufactured in Starville. Major Dankworth had recently declared that on behalf of Starville city's revenue he would be adding an extra tariff on any products produced in his city which were sold outside of it.

The Birdwhistle's business made little enough profit as it was. Aiden was not even sure it was legal to inflict increased tariffs on inventory produced in the same country let alone the same state. Since he was the public face of the family business, Aiden told his dad that he was happy to go plead their case with Mayor Dankworth in hopes that the Mayor would see the importance of keeping local products marketable at a competitive price. Even though *Sunbeams in a Box*'s headquarters was in Sunlight City, both cities benefited from the business. Adding extra tariffs sounded like something the mafia would do, not legitimate business partners who both gained something from the arrangement. Aiden had headed to the meeting with a positive outlook that he could convince the Mayor to see his side of the situation logically...until he found the man dead. What were the chances of that?

Aiden was glad it had not been his aging father who found the body, the shock might have killed him too. He was also relieved that his younger brother had not accompanied him this trip, the sight was too gruesome. What was he talking about? Both male Birdwhistles would probably have handled it better than he had and not run off like a freaked-out little kid. Aiden mulled over returning to the scene of the crime but decided it was too late. It had been over an hour since he had driven off like a bat out of Hades. The body had likely been discovered by now. And if he didn't slow down the police were going to pick him up regardless of whether he called them about the corpse or not. Maybe he should go back after all. What was his best option?

Aiden drove down to Starville once a week in the work truck to pick up a new supply of solar panels from the factory. This was the first time he had scheduled a meeting beforehand with the Mayor. His family was just so frustrated by the new fees that would have such an adverse effect on their small business. Aiden determined that he needed to try to talk some sense into the man. What were the odds that the Mayor would not be alive to listen? Someone else was obviously frustrated with the guy too. Aiden hit the brakes; he had forgotten to pick up the panels.

Before turning the truck around, Aiden decided to flip on the radio as he continued up the mountain. He was not too far outside of Moonburg. He should still have enough reception to be able to pick up a local station to see if he could hear any news bulletins. Bad news travels fast so it might be keeping up with him. Should he call his dad and let him know what had happened? No, no need to worry them yet. This kind of news was better given in person anyway.

It was a few minutes before the top of the hour, so he listened to the end of *Bad, Bad Leroy Brown* on the oldies station before a woman with a British or maybe it was an

Australian accent came over the airwaves to announce the news. Perhaps KJOY radio station felt that this woman's voice made even the dullest news more interesting to listen to. They could be right. She started off with a few items from the national news, then shared some sports scores and gave a traffic update. Maybe he was in the clear. Aiden was ready to listen to the next golden oldie when the woman with the accent continued, "Sad news just in, Mayor Dankworth of Starville has been found dead this morning in his office of an apparent homicide. The police are searching for a person of interest. The man is believed to be in his twenties and driving a yellow pickup truck with the words *Sunbeams in a Box* across the side. If you see this truck please contact the police, the suspect may be armed and dangerous."

A sudden wave of sickness washed over him, and Aiden felt like he was going to vomit. He might as well be driving a bright flashing neon sign with the words "I'm the suspect," tattooed on his forehead. What should he do now? The obvious and probably the best thing to do was to turn around and go back to Starville. He was innocent and could logically explain it all to the police. He would not come across as a murderer. Would he? He did touch the body to check the pulse, so his prints were probably at the scene.

Aiden began to slow down so he could flip a U-turn, when out of nowhere a dog dashed in front of his truck. He swerved to miss the dog but had not slowed enough to maintain control. The truck lurched off of the road and down an embankment before coming to rest with a crunch against a substantial tree trunk. Aiden's head bounced off the windshield and his airbag deployed. An unpleasant chemical smell most likely from the airbag filled his nostrils. His seatbelt had held him snuggly in place, and he was still conscious. This was definitely not his day. The truck was not going anywhere on its own in the near future, whether back to Starville or home. The engine appeared to be partially jammed up into the interior of the cab and the hood of the truck was crunched open with steam rising from something beneath it that had probably been punctured.

The first thought that flashed through his mind was, "Had he hit the dog? Was he going to be accused of two murders in one single morning?" The door of the truck still opened thank, Zeus. Aiden shoved the heavy metal uphill and stiffly dropped down from the truck. Where was he? And where was that dog?

If he had driven off of the highway only a few miles earlier, he wouldn't have hit this big tree. The vegetation had begun to change in the last bit of the drive becoming more like his upper mountain landscaping. The ground cover was denser than he expected as he forged through the forested area looking for the dog he may have hit. Why did he care? Maybe Aiden had hit his head harder than he thought he had and was a bit deranged. It was doubtful the dog belonged to anyone up here. Maybe it was a wild dog or even a wolf that would attack him if they ran into each other. Injured animals could be unpredictable. Aiden just did not want another living thing bleeding out on him this morning. He pushed aside more limbs heading deeper into the foliage away from the road. Watch him get himself lost on top of everything else.

Thinking that he heard a noise to the right Aiden made his way around a rock formation and spotted the animal in question. The dog appeared tame, Aiden was pretty sure, and the canine looked to be intact without apparent injuries, but Aiden's eyes did not examine the beast thoroughly. The sight just beyond the dog totally captured and redirected Aiden's attention. He must definitely have a head injury and be hallucinating. In front of him, looming overhead stood the largest tree that he had ever seen in this area with a structure of some sort built up among the branches. It appeared to Aiden, the now suspected murderer, and possible dog hitter, that he had happened upon an abode inspired by the Swiss Family Robinson's home.

Chapter 2

The Sun is a big ball of gas and plasma. Almost three-quarters are composed of hydrogen (over 70%), whilst most of the remaining mass is helium (24-28%). The other elements (approximately 2%) include trace amounts of iron, nickel, oxygen, and all the other elements found in the Solar System. The hydrogen is converted into energy in the sun's core. This energy moves outward through the interior layers into the sun's atmosphere and is released into the solar system as heat and light. There are some amazingly large and bright stars, like Eta Carinae and Betelgeuse, but they are incredibly far away. Our own Sun is a relatively bright star when comparing the 50 closest stars located within 17 light-years of the Earth. In absolute terms, the Sun would be the 4th brightest of those stars.

Luna

Sherlock came bounding into view. Her dog had been off exploring. Luna did not keep him leashed out here in the woods and something seemed to have gotten him all worked upon his most recent adventure. Luna Fernsby was a thirtyishyear-old woman who in a few years would be edging closer to forty than thirty. She grew up in Moonburg but was not as academically minded as most of the people who dwelt there. The major premises she lived her life by were based upon things of a more spiritual nature and how she felt inside. She may not have been literally run out of town with a pitchfork, but she might as well have been. Luna was not included in any social events back in Moonburg. The kids in high school and eventually college had suggested that the root of her name was derived from the word lunatic when in reality her college professor parents had named her for the Roman goddess of the moon which was extremely logical considering the name of the town where she was born. Luna was more comfortable living outside of the city limits anyway.

On one of her hikes into the foothills over seven years ago, she had discovered a unique and unusually large tree. Its branches divided down the center like the part in a person's hair. About eight feet up from the base of the trunk they grew out almost horizontally for several feet before turning skyward again. Luna could envision a small home sitting comfortably in the heart of the tree almost like a nest for a huge bird or possibly for an average-sized woman who didn't fly with wings but whose mind soared often to unusual heights. That is how Luna came to live in a treehouse which of course added to the legend of her less than stable or even addled mind.

Her by far best and pretty much only friend, Pax, had tried to get her to move back into town for years. His weekly visits brought a touch of humanity into her existence as well as other more practical supplies. On one visit he had come bearing a puppy insisting it was for her safety since he couldn't be near at all times to protect her. Pax felt that she needed a watchdog and daily companionship. There had been a momentary dilemma on how a dog could live in a tree. Then Pax had built a ramp for the dog. The little guy took a while to get used to it as a puppy. In the meantime, she had had to carry him up the ramp, but now he bounded up the plank without hesitation. Thank goodness he gained the skill before reaching his full weight of nearly ninety pounds. Now she could almost ride him up the ramp if she wanted to.

Luna's bicycle with large saddlebags hanging over each side was leaning against the base of the tree for emergency trips into town when needed and an old-fashioned icebox kept perishables fresh between Pax's visits. Her life was delightfully simple. She lived like she was permanently camping, maybe more like glamping. She had all the basic comforts of home. Propane lights and stove kept her warm, allowed for hot meals, and enabled her to work after the sun went down whenever necessary. It was easy to rise and go to bed with the sun. People had done it for centuries before, but backup lighting was nice.

There was a fresh stream nearby with water available for washing and cleaning. Luna preferred to use bottled water for drinking and cooking just in case giardia or other bacteria were present, and bottled water saved her from having to boil everything she consumed. The one convenience she had not fully perfected was the bathroom situation. She had rigged up an outdoor shower, but it was difficult to keep the water at a comfortable temperature for very long. As an alternate bathing option and always during the winter months she heated water on the propane burner for a bath in her tin tub. If she pined for a long soak in a porcelain tub or the weather was too cold for an outdoor shower, her friend in town was always willing to share his plumbed facilities. An old-fashion outhouse with a compost toilet served as a rustic porta-potty for her elimination needs. She had developed her own hygienic system that honestly could use improvement. Maybe for her birthday, she would ask Pax for an indoor camping toilet. They weren't as expensive as composting ones, and it would be wonderful not having to go outside to pee on frosty mornings.

She was brought back to the present by Sherlock's whine. The dog was not behaving like himself. Luna headed over to take a closer look when she noticed a young man, at least younger than herself which made her less afraid of him for some strange reason, standing just outside their clearing. Blood from a head wound was dripping into his eyes as he emerged from the trees and stumbled into the unmarked perimeter of the property that she had claimed as her own. His blonde bangs looked as if they had been dyed an ombre-dipped pink as he brushed the blood back into his hair with his forearm. Luna felt a bolt of adrenaline-laced energy rush through her body, she was not really scared, more startled with a dash of curiosity. She swallowed a small shriek before it escaped her lips.

The unidentified man spoke first to quickly clarify his surprise visit. "I just wanted to make sure the dog was alright. I was afraid I may have hit him with my truck."

"It looks like my dog is doing just fine, thanks. I cannot say the same about you, however. You look pretty banged up. Are you okay?" Luna was much more worried about the man in front of her than her dog. Sherlock seemed perfectly fine physically, he was just displaying his purpose, a heightened protectiveness due to the intruder's presence.

"I think I'm okay," the man answered even though he looked a little wobbly on his feet, "maybe I do need to sit down for a minute. It's been a weird morning."

Luna guessed the newcomer must have been in some kind of accident and might be in shock. What should she do? Warm him up and get blood to his head she thought she remembered from a first aid course. "Would you like some tea?" Tea was warm.

"Do you have anything stronger?"

It appeared the guy was not going to be shy. "No, not really, but I do blend my own tea and it packs a pretty good punch. It might make you feel better right now." She could invite him up to her second-story chateau to recover but she knew nothing about the man so pushed a patio chair forward for him to drop into. Luna used the term patio loosely. She had gathered enough flat rocks to form a faux paver-stone area with a firepit for outdoor entertaining and enjoyment. It was not Better Homes and Gardens worthy but worked.

"Thanks. I'd appreciate a cup. And maybe a little time to sort out the puzzle in my head."

Luna was still worried about his injury but not sure how much to pry. "I'll bring you a wet cloth too. To wipe yourself up with. I could call for real medical assistance. You know, to make sure there isn't bleeding inside your head as well as outside of it," She offered.

The man seemed to have forgotten about the bleeding and touched his forehead again looking surprised to see redness on his fingers. "No, I'm fine. I just need to sit for a bit and get my bearings. You can check my pupils to make sure they're even-sized if it makes you feel better. And if I pass out, you can call someone I guess."

Luna glanced into his cerulean blue eyes before going to brew the tea. They looked normal to her in the equally-dilated-pupils aspect anyway. The man was pretty cavalier about his injury. She was not sure if he was being stoic or stupid, so it was difficult to determine the best plan of action moving forward. She would start with the tea and wet cloth and go from there.

"Here you go. Homegrown, or more home gathered and brewed. See if you can pick out any flavors." Luna handed the man whose name she didn't even know the mug and dishrag, "My name is Luna by the way."

"I'm Aiden. Thanks again," he responded.

That was it? She needed more info. "Not trying to be nosy, but what happened?"

"Probably the less you know about me the better. I was driving home and saw your dog on the road. I swerved to miss him, glad he is okay by the way, but couldn't miss the tree afterward when I went off the road." He took a swig of the tea, "I'm not really a tea man, but this is decent. I think I detect a hint of pine and something bitter? Don't really know tea flavors. Hopefully, it isn't hemlock laced for your uninvited intruder out here in the backwoods."

Luna laughed. If the man, she now knew to be Aiden, still had a sense of humor his head injury must not be too bad. "I think poison-hemlock is supposed to taste somewhat like parsnip and has a mouse-like smell. No, I haven't poisoned you yet. The bitter flavor you taste is probably dandelion and there is some ginger root for the zing. You did pick up the pine. Good job. Now what else can I do for you?" She wanted to add, "before I send you on your way", but didn't want to come across rude. Aiden seemed pretty harmless. And after all, he had been injured protecting her errant dog from being run over. Sherlock seemed to be comfortable with him now and dogs were supposedly good judges of character. She was just not sure of the guy's intentions. Why it was better that she "not know much about him"?

"If you're really offering and I could be so bold as to ask…I'd really appreciate being allowed to hang out here for a while. Maybe a day or so. I'll reimburse you for any food or anything else you'd like me to, even pay for the campsite. I don't have to stay up in your treehouse, although it does look amazing, if you have a sleeping bag that I could borrow that'd be great. I'm sure the nights get cold."

Whoa, bold was putting it mildly. This guy was a certifiable wacko and that was coming from a suspected lunatic. There was definitely more to his story and now Luna was in a predicament. How could she get him to leave? Sherlock did not look like he was going to be any help. The two of them were getting chummy as Aiden scratched her dog behind his ears. Pax was not due for another day. She may have to call Pax and ask him to come earlier or maybe she should call the police. When she didn't answer immediately Aiden went on.

"I know my request must sound insane to you. Before you call the cops on me please give me a chance. I did spare your dog. I wish I could share more, but truly it's best this way. Just one day is all I ask. Then I will get out of your hair. I promise." The guy pleaded, looking pathetic with his battered face, blood-smeared hair, and large blue eyes.

What could she say? No, she should definitely say no, but out of her mouth came, "I don't feel great about this and I do have a gun that I am not afraid to use," she failed to mention it was only a BB gun to scare off any unwanted varmints and predators. Hopefully, he wouldn't join that category. "I will give you one day to figure out this 'puzzle in your head' that you mentioned, then you have to go. But no funny business."

"Yes, thank you. No funny business. And I promise to go soon. My life is just a little messed up right now. You're an angel."

Being called an angel was better than being called a lunatic, but Luna knew she was neither. If she got a bad feeling about her guest, she would call the police regardless of what she had told him. But for some unexplainable reason, she actually did feel okay about letting Aiden stay.

Chapter 3

__About one million Earths could fit inside the Sun.__ A hollow Sun would fit approximately 960,000 spherical Earths and if squished with no wasted space, then around 1,300,000 Earth's would fit inside. The Sun's surface area is 11,990 times that of the Earth's surface area, it is 109 times wider than the Earth and its overall mass is approximately 330,000 times greater than that of Earth. To put its size in perspective, the Sun's mass constitutes 99.86% of the mass of our entire Solar System. Yet, there are much bigger sun/stars out there. The biggest star that we know of would almost reach Saturn if it were to replace our Sun inside of our Solar System.

Pax

Saturdays were Pax Loughty's favorite day of the week. Not because he was off of work, although that was great, but because he got to spend most of the day with Luna. She was smart, funny, creative, beautiful and he had loved her for at least ten years. However, Luna appeared to be totally oblivious of his fermenting feelings. How could she not know? Did the girl who made his heart beat faster think he was just hanging out with her like a big brother being his sister's keeper? He was kind and an okay-looking guy. Did she have even a drop of non-platonic interest in him? She had certainly friend-zoned him, and Pax was deathly afraid to break out of that tidy box. A friend Luna was better than no Luna.

Maybe she disregarded the more-than-friends-option because he still lived in his childhood home with his mother. His mom was getting older and needed someone there with her. Since Pax was not living with anyone else, it was convenient for both him and his mom. He had invited Luna more than once to move in with them. His mother would be totally okay with the arrangement, she didn't want to hold Pax back from moving on in his life. Perhaps the co-living option wasn't as appealing to Luna. There was already one Mrs. Loughty in the house, so the scenario could lend credibility to the little sister and not romantic interest notion. Pax didn't think he was afraid to openly pursue a permanent relationship but keeping mom in the equation could be a safety net. He just wanted to be a good guy for both of the women in his life. For now, he would continue to be Luna's connection to the city and work towards the real connection he wanted.

Five years before, Pax had picked out a labradoodle for Luna. A breed large enough to be a decent watchdog or protector and it didn't shed. Not that shedding mattered out in the forest, but if he ever did convince her to move in with him the shed-free factor would be a good trait to have in their sort of co-owned dog. It had been a gift for Luna, but he shared in the responsibility whenever needed. They had named the dog together so that could be considered relationship forwarding behavior, couldn't it? The team action had given Pax a possibly delusional hope in a future together at some point with their co-named pet. The dog was obviously far more attached to Luna, but Pax was full-time backup caregiver and shared custody on weekends.

They had considered puppy names for a few weeks. The first one they tried out was Puck from Shakespeare's *Midsummer's Night Dream* since as a puppy the dog was mischievous and had made them both fall magically in love with him, but for some reason, the moniker didn't quite fit. Quixote was their next consideration. Don Quixote from *Man of La Mancha* was chivalrous, and the canine could be Luna's knight in shining armor. But the fictional character was also an unrealistic, idealist dreamer and they hoped that the dog would be a more practical companion for Luna since she lived alone. Then the perfect fit came to mind. They both loved

Sherlock Holmes mysteries. The dog showed great perceptiveness and liked to investigate everything around him. Their third choice was the charm, and the black labradoodle puppy was aptly dubbed Sir Sherlock. Sherlock was not a puppy anymore. Time was passing, Pax needed to make his intentions more clear before it became time to get Luna a second dog to name and share custody of.

Thoughts of how he might advance and eventually achieve the desire of his heart did not come easily as he drove the ten minutes out of town and turned off onto the dirt lane that led to her tree. Pax didn't find the tree living odd, in fact, he liked that about Luna. He would be happy to live there with her on weekends if she preferred. He was getting to the point he would live anywhere with her. He may even need to consider the "M" word at some point…going all-in with full-on commitment.

The tree which held her house came into view. Naturally colored roughhewn wood formed two small rooms surrounded by the tree limbs. Each room had a glass window looking out of the front to greet him. Behind one window was a living room/kitchen combo, the other was Luna's bedroom if you could call it that. The privacy space was wall to wall bed. A peaked shake shingle roof housed the loft where Luna did much of the work for her business and a wooden railing ran across the front of the home surrounding a small deck area. The place really was quite charming and fit perfectly almost camouflaged within the tree. During the winter when the leaves were gone the little home was more obvious or visible. Today it looked just perfect tucked away in the tree with his Rapunzel inside. That is until Pax's eyes wandered down below the treehouse to the left of the ramp he had built for Sherlock. There stretched out in a chair on the rock patio was a man who looked far too at home poaching a place in Pax's world.

Feeling an unpleasant mixture of horror and jealousy, Pax wondered what in the heck had happened in the week he was away as he jumped from his SUV. Perhaps he needed to call daily to keep closer tabs on his woman and prevent errant claim jumpers. He called out to Luna, but the man in the chair answered.

"Sorry, Luna isn't here, she and Sherlock went off on a walk looking for more ingredients to make new flavors of tea. Can I help you?"

There were so many things wrong with that answer that Pax didn't know where to begin. First, the guy could help him by leaving. How did he know that Luna made specialty teas and what her dog's name was? This guy had obviously been here a while. He was handsome enough. And even though the mystery man must be almost ten years younger than Luna, she was fun, youthful and a catch for any age.

"I come every Saturday and bring Luna's supplies," lame, lame, lame reply.

"Oh, you're the grocery guy. I'm sure she won't be long."

The grocery guy?! That is what he had become to her. Ouch. "Actually, Luna and I go way back, and I don't think she has ever mentioned you." Pax needed to salvage some dignity.

"That's Aiden," Luna offered as she walked up. "He's a new friend that I've recently became acquainted with when he almost hit Sherlock." The dog hearing his name came into their circle and wandered over to the new guy for a rub down. The traitor dog even liked him.

"So, since he almost hits the dog, he moves in?" Pax tried to come across as joking and not as annoyed as he actually felt. Luna's petite frame standing in front of him with green eyes ablaze, freckle-splattered nose, and thick auburn hair which would not remain confined to its messy bun made his heart melt.

"Well, of course, there's more to the story..." Aiden interrupted Luna and finished her explanation, "there always is. I was injured in the process and Luna let me recover for a few days."

The story just kept getting worse. Wait, Aiden. That name sounded familiar. "Did you say your name is Aiden. As in Aiden Birdwhistle?"

"I didn't give a last name, but yes, that is my name." Aiden answered easily.

"Luna could I talk to you privately for a few minutes?" Pax asked.

"Pax, I don't want to be rude. I'm sure you can ask me in front of Aiden."

"I really cannot." Pax was insistent.

"We'll just be a few minutes, Aiden. Please excuse us." Luna looked a little put out as Pax pulled her aside.

"Luna, that guy's name has been plastered all over the news. He's wanted for murder."

"Don't be ridiculous, Aiden is harmless. He was even worried about hitting a dog," Luna scoffed. "Is this the competitive male coming out in you? Not sure that I like it."

"I promise, I'm not being ridiculous. Do you know anything about the guy? Let's just ask him and see how he reacts," Pax felt a little too happy about the possible turn of events, but if the guy was a wanted killer it did lessen the competition.

"Fine, do what you must, but don't be a jerk about it."
Luna requested.

Aiden already looked a little uneasy when they reapproached and spoke up first. "I think I may know what this is all about."

"I bet you do. Your name has been all over the local news. Can you explain yourself?" Pax didn't want to directly accuse the guy of murder and possibly end up his next victim.

"Wait, Aiden, is that the puzzle you had to figure out? Did you kill someone?" Luna's voice raised.

"No, I definitely did not kill anyone. I promise. But some people think I did." Aiden admitted.

"And why would they think that if you didn't?" Pax pressed.

"Well, I did have an appointment with the man, but I found him already dead. I freaked out and took off. I was turning around to go back and explain when I thought I hit Sherlock and then did hit the tree."

"Who did you supposedly kill?" Luna interrupted.

"Mayor Dankworth of Starville unfortunately."

"You need to leave immediately. Do you realize the position you've put Luna in!? She has been harboring a fugitive." Pax was visibly distressed. And the guy could still be a killer, although Pax had his doubts. Either way, Luna was as oblivious to the danger that she had put herself into as she was to the crush from one or maybe even both of the men in the clearing.

"Pax, he didn't tell me anything so that I wouldn't be an accomplice. I think he needs our help," Luna countered. "Remember innocent until proven guilty?"

"No, Pax is right. It's just a matter of time before they find my truck and then your place by proximity. It's probably time I turn myself in."

Chapter 4

*__The Sun is middle-aged so approximately halfway
through its lifespan.__ The Sun is a second-generation
star which means it is partly made from other stars. It is
currently 4.7 billion years old and has already burned off
about half of its store of hydrogen. The Sun has enough
hydrogen left to continue to burn for approximately another 5
billion more years. In its current phase, the Sun is a type of
star known as a main-sequence G2V star or a Yellow Dwarf.*

Zori

Mayor Dankworth was dead, and Zori was not sad
about it. The face that Starville's Mayor presented to the world
was one of a model citizen but Zori knew differently. The man
had undercover business dealings that were quite dirty and
even revolting. When she heard that an Aiden Birdwhistle was
suspected of the crime, her first thought was good for him.
Then Zori's second thought which followed immediately
afterward was that she was pretty positive the accused Mr.

Birdwhistle did not do it. The murder was committed by someone far closer to home. She knew for a fact that a few of the dead Mayor's less than aboveboard business dealings happened to be with her father, Marcus MacQuiod. He would be a much more likely suspect. Zori had known for some time that her dad's business was not totally on the up and up and that the Mayor and her dad had behind-the-scenes deals going on. However, she never foresaw this outcome.

Zori lived in Starville and had for all twenty-two years of her young life, but she had never loved the dimness of the city. That was the best way to describe it. Her hometown never felt bright to her. She knew her that father ran nefarious businesses behind the front of his fairly legitimate car dealership MacQuiod Motors, but what was a daughter to do...turn her dad in? She didn't know all the details. She tried not to get involved and made an effort to stay above the squalor that surrounded her, but she had ended up in an awful situation.

Zori worked for her dad at MacQuiod Motors doing whatever job was needed at the moment...at the parts and service counter, in accounts payable, on the showroom floor, or as a ride-along on test drives for their customers. She knew pretty much everything that went on from opening to close. The after hour high-stakes poker games were good clean fun compared to other things she had witnessed. Zori was pretty sure legal imports would not be transported in the wheel wells or under seat cushions of the vehicles they purchased. It did not take an Einstein to realize that drugs were being trafficked through their car dealership. Then she did not even want to guess what kind of employment the artificially attractive, gaudily dressed, garishly made-up women with humongous bosoms were applying for in her father's office. At times it was better to look the other way and not know.

The likely innocent Mr. Birdwhistle needed to run fast or fly far away. The man sounded like a decent person from the news briefings. And decent people didn't usually resort to murder, yet there was always a first. He had to at least have developed a sense of humor with a last name like his. The guy could have finally snapped from one too many Birdwhistle jokes. Aiden, that was his first name, appeared to be quite fine-looking from his photos. The news stations were running his picture every hour across the television screen in special news reports for people to keep their eyes open for the missing man. There was one shot from his senior yearbook wearing a sports coat and tie, and another in a tracksuit. Zori noticed his nice legs and muscular arms. He had been a star athlete at Sunlight High School five years ago turning down a track and field scholarship for pole vault to work in the family solar business.

She wondered what had gone wrong in the guy's life these last few years since high school to make him a murder suspect.

Zori had graduated from Star High School three years ago and was also working in the family business. They had that in common. She had missed a lot of school the year her mother left so had had to repeat the third grade and didn't graduate until she was nineteen. Although older than most of the others who were graduating and going off to college, she still didn't know what she wanted to do with her life so her father had told her she could work at the dealership until she figured it out.

It was that she wasn't smart. Although in all honesty, she probably had more street smarts than book smarts. Still, Zori wanted to do something valuable with her life and find a niche that gave her purpose. Who didn't? She started driving to Moonburg one night a week and taking a class each semester at the college there. Last semester she had taken a course on booking keeping to enhance her skills for the business. However, to prevent her father from ever asking her to doctor their books, she decided to keep her knowledge in that arena mediocre.

This semester she was taking a class for her own enjoyment. One that she was actually interested in and excited about. She alternated between practical and pleasurable courses and it was her turn to attend for fun. The course was in the culinary department… Baking 201. Zori loved to bake and watched a ton of cooking and bake-off shows on TV so had decided to skip Baking 101. She was starting to think that baking might be her niche. Maybe one day her dad would let her open a small bakery on a pad next to the car dealership if she got good enough. Even better, perhaps he could float her a loan or fund her in opening a shop further away from his influence. With backgrounds in both cooking and budgeting, she was on the right track to run her own business.

Zori began baking cookies in her teens. She had made every variety of cookie recipe she could find and perfected her favorites…frosted sugar, snickerdoodle, and all variations of chocolate chip even adding pumpkin in the autumn. Her neighbors and employees at the car dealership benefitted from sampling her wares. From cookies, she moved on to cupcakes with unique fillings and frostings. For a while, she thought she might like to have a cupcake shop or even a cupcake trailer. It did not seem like it would be too difficult to convert one of the older vans on the lot into space to market her cupcakes to potential car customers. Or perhaps with the purchase of a car the new owner could drive away with a dozen cupcakes as a bonus. Her marketing ideas were endless, but she had yet to share any of them with her father.

Lately she had started baking cakes. The base ingredients were similar to cupcakes, so the transition was easy. There was just so much more one could do artistically with the whole canvas of a cake top and sides. Zori had been studying themes of ones she would like to create one day. She made a simple star cake to start, next she baked a rainbow cake with each of the six layers a different brilliant color of the rainbow and a sun partially obscured by a cloud on top. It was time to break out of the solar system themes. Maybe a garden bouquet with many types of flowers splattered across the top would be lovely or a cake with cars on top for the dealership. Her mind floated to other exotic cake options as she performed her menial tasks. Zori would love to be in a real bake-off competition at some point if she got good enough.

The soft rock music over the MacQuiod Motors intercom system paused for the radio announcer to interject a news bulletin with an update on the Mayor's murder investigation. "…I am unable to show you, listeners, a photo of the suspect who has disappeared, but the authorities also need your help locating his vehicle which is missing as well…" Then the DJ gave the description of the truck he was last seen driving. A big yellow vehicle with *Sunbeams in a Box* scrawled across the side didn't seem like it would be too difficult to spot. The police should probably check with local car dealerships to see if any trucks had been repainted recently. Maybe Zori should be a detective. Perhaps criminology could be her next class, it would be both practical and interesting. She was super curious about this guy so would have to dig deeper and see what she could find out about him. It would be cool if she could find him before the authorities did. She would tell him she knew he was innocent and to leave the country. Why would he listen to her? No one else listened to her.

She wished with all of her heart, for the millionth time, that her mother had not left her. People listened to her mother, well, everyone except her father. And her mom would know the right thing to do, much more than her dad did anyway. Zori would have left with her mom if her mother had let her. Vada MacQuoid told Zori that she could not go, that she would be better off here. How could that be? Zori wanted to stay with her mother, but Vada insisted that her young daughter needed to stay and help her father. Look how that had turned out. Zori still spoke with her mom regularly and received some guidance, but her mother had moved too far away for shared custody or even holiday visits as a little girl. It was like they were in different worlds and conversing occasionally was not the same as having her mom close.

Try as hard as she might, Zori couldn't remember many specifics about her mother. They must look a lot alike because people were always telling her that she looked just like her mother or that her mother had been as strikingly fair as she was. When Zori looked into the mirror, she tried to see her mother's face, not hers. She knew that her mother liked birds, clouds, and stars or astronomy, most things in the heavens it seemed if the few trinkets she had left behind were any indication. Whenever she asked, Zori's father would share with Zori the story of how her parents had met at an Indie band concert, though the band was no longer making music. Vada had been loudly singing along with every song as if no one was listening and had had such an angelic voice that he had wanted to wrap her up and take her home with him. Eventually, he did.

Mother Vada could have at least left Zori with a sibling. Instead, Vada had left Zori with her face, the name she had bestowed upon her and that was pretty much it, besides two children's books with handwritten notes inscribed inside the covers. One was *How to Catch a Star* by Oliver Jeffers. Zori's real name Zoriah meant "star" in Slavic. She was named for the low light orb and their low-life city which she only wanted to escape as soon as she could. The story however was sweet. A little boy struggled to catch a star and finally found one in a different way than the reader supposed he would. Maybe there was a more adult analogy in it somewhere for her to discover one day.

The other book was *I'll Love You to the Moon and Back* by Amelia Hepworth. Most of the things that the mother bear did with her cub in the story were things that Zori may have done with her own mother when she was little but didn't remember and could not do with her now. It did talk about different ways a person could show their love. Zori had learned to be creative in that category; it was much easier expressing love when the person was with you. Towards the end, a page reminded the reader that *our love is always with us and it never ends*. Her mom probably thought these books would have meaning for her daughter. But Zori's mom felt further away than the moon most days and Zori would rather have her here than any book.

Forcing herself not to dwell on all that she didn't have, Zori turned her thoughts back to her next project for Baking 201…a three-layer cake with ganache between the layers and fondant frosting…there were so many combinations to consider. Intermixing with her cake creation possibilities were overlaying ideas of what she could possibly do to find Mr. Aiden Birdwhistle. It was going to be an okay day in the dealership today, her body may be here working, but her mind was off on more stimulating adventures of its own.

Chapter 5

Many ancient civilizations have centered their culture and religion around the Sun. The Aztecs worshipped the sun gods Tonatiuh and Huitzilopochtli, the Incas the sun god Int, the Egyptians sun god Ra, the Greeks the sun gods Helios and Apollo, the Japanese sun goddess Amaterasu, and there are many more examples. The sun gods of the Aztec religion demanded regular human sacrifices.

Aiden

The natural environment was so peaceful. Leaves rustled overhead and rays of sun scattered light across the paver stones. The last day had been a respite from whatever lay ahead of him. Aiden longed to stay in this sheltered bubble and pretend what had happened had not. But the longer he stayed the worse it would look, the angstier those looking for him would become and the more vulnerable those sheltering him would be to accountability. Yes, it was time for him to stand up as a man and face the music or maybe face the firing squad was a more appropriate metaphor. He was not an English major, so he was not really sure.

"You've been more than hospitable Miss Luna Fernsby. Thank you. I appreciate all of the tending to. I think I'm even starting to tolerate tea. But I believe it's time for me to say adieu. However, there's one small hiccup, I lack a set of drivable wheels at the moment. Can I ask for one last favor? Possibly a ride into town? There may even be a bounty on my head that you could collect. Or if a ride isn't possible, directions to give an Uber or Lift driver would be helpful. You're a tad off the grid and I'm virtually lost." Aiden gave his impromptu farewell speech.

"If you insist on turning yourself in, of course, I'll give you a ride, but I'm going too. The authorities might not believe your story." Luna insisted. His female rescuer must have gained some invested concern for him over the past twenty-four-plus hours.

"And how are you going to drive him to town? On the handlebars of your bike?" Pax pointed out. "I can take him down in my SUV and drop him off at the police station."

"I'm going with you then." Pax did not look pleased but did not say no to Luna.

Aiden went to gather his belongings and realized he had left them all in his truck, even his phone which would be completely dead by now.

"I lied," Aiden realized Pax probably thought he meant about the murder as he continued on, "I left my phone in my truck and should probably let my family know that I am alive and that I didn't kill anyone. One more favor, can I borrow a phone?"

Begrudgingly Pax handed over his phone to Aiden who immediately dialed his home phone number not knowing who if anyone would answer. His little brother's deepening voice came over the line, not sounding so little anymore, "Hello, Birdwhistle's residence." Their mother had trained them to answer the phone respectfully and even suggested that they could add a little whistle at the end of the salutation which both brothers adamantly refused to do. Luckily most of their friends called their cell phones so the formal greeting was not a problem.

"Rocco, this is Aiden."

"Whoa bro, where are you? All shiz is breaking loose up here."

"I know. Sorry. I'm okay and I'm going to turn myself in. Just tell mom and dad I didn't do it." Aiden asked.

"Duh, we assumed, but you gotta give me more info than that. Where've you been and what in the hallelujah happened?" Rocco queried. Their mother also insisted there be no swearing in their home, so his brother had gotten quite creative with his expletives.

"I'll explain more later. I've been hanging out in the woods just beyond the moor and am on a borrowed phone. If any of you want to see me, I'm headed to the Moonburg police station. And tell dad sorry, I wrecked the truck and may need bail money. Thanks, bud." Aiden returned the phone to Pax.

"I would hate receiving a call like that," Luna admitted.

The trio climbed into Pax's army green SUV. Aiden noticed Luna didn't lock Sherlock up in the treehouse when they left. The dog must be good about staying around home except when dashing in front of his truck. Perhaps other forces had been at work to bring him to their treehouse. They drove in silence. Aiden felt his chest constrict as if holding his breath. The road on the way back to Moonburg looked far different than the drive through yesterday and he had no idea what was waiting in front of him when he returned. He had crawled into the backseat letting the friends ride up front together. His backseat location added to the fugitive feeling as he watched the two front-seat passengers exchange glances at each other but not know what to say. All the car needed was bars or plexiglass between the two rows and he would be arriving at the station in a dang paddy wagon.

There were a few reporters milling around the cement steps that led into the building trolling for the latest news scoop when they pulled up. Well, the story had arrived, he was here. Who would have guessed he'd become such a newsworthy nugget? No doubt many more media reps with cameras and note pads would be joining this lot soon. As Aiden stepped from the vehicle there was a brief hesitation before he was recognized and surrounded by the meager paparazzi crew. Aiden strode between the camera bearers casting them the solo comment, "I will give my statement and anything else I have to say inside."

Aiden's entourage stayed protectively close, Luna trailing him through the front doors and Pax who was not about to leave Luna followed behind. Aiden's two sidekicks were relegated to a bench against the wall to wait and deflect the reporter's questions as a large office ushered Aiden into his office. Aiden couldn't tell if this guy was going to assume the role of good cop or bad cop with him, but his first impressions definitely did not come across as friendly. The man was about the age of his father, minus his dad's smile lines or any impression of good humor. His uniform fit snuggly through the midsection but there were outlines of residual strength through his chest and shoulders. The badge over his left pocket displayed the name Sallow on it. However, the guy's complexion was not what Aiden would call sallow; his skin had an uneven ruddy appearance with large pores across his nose. Officer Sallow probably packed away a few brews at the local bar after hours. Aiden would not judge the man for needing to unwind from his stressful job after work.

"We've been searching for you Mr. Birdwhistle," Officer Sallow stated. "You've had my men on the hunt."

"Yes, I've heard. I wrecked my truck and was temporarily out of commission," Aiden hedged the full truth.

"I assume you're aware why you're wanted." Officer Sallow stated plainly.

"I have a pretty good idea, but you have the wrong man." Aiden lamely replied.

"I've heard that one before, are you denying you were with Mayor Dankworth early yesterday morning. We've not determined the exact time of his death."

"No, I admit I was there, but the man was already dead. I know I shouldn't have taken off, but I must have been in shock." Hopefully, that speculation would explain his errant behavior.

"I'll need to get a full statement from you. Then we'll hold you here while we gather further evidence." The officer informed him.

"Hold me for how long? What about bail?"

"I'm not sure how long you'll be our resident. Possibly for life, whether here or in a penitentiary, if convicted. I'm going to recommend no bail to the judge. You've already demonstrated yourself a flight risk and we've no other suspects at this time."

This was not happening. Someone had to be able to talk some sense into Officer Sallow. Aiden was innocent. "The people who brought me here can vouch for me, at least the woman can. I showed up at her place yesterday after my wreck. She didn't know who I was and doesn't have a car. Her friend, that guy out there, drove me here today. Talk to them." His argument sounded weak even to himself.

"Mr. Birdwhistle, unless you have an eyewitness that was with you when you *supposedly* found Mayor Dankworth already dead, you're not going anywhere." With that, Swallow left Aiden sitting in his office as he called for another officer to escort Aiden to a holding cell for the time being.

Aiden wasn't sure what he had thought would happen when he turned himself in, but this definitely wasn't what he had pictured. As he was led down the hallway in handcuffs past Luna and Pax, all he could think to say was, "Thanks for the ride guys," before he was shoved into a six-by-eight cell and locked up with a key. He had traded Luna's forest retreat for cement and steel. Aiden Birdwhistle had become a different kind of bird, one without a song...he was now a jailbird.

Chapter 6

Light from the Sun takes eight minutes to reach Earth. The Sun is an average distance of 150 million kilometers from the Earth and light travels at 300,000 kilometers per second. Dividing one by the other gives us an approximate time of 500 seconds or eight minutes and 20 seconds. Although this energy reaches Earth in a few minutes, it will already have taken millions of years to travel from the Sun's core to its surface.

Luna / Pax

Luna was not sure what to do. She certainly hadn't been much help at the police station. After getting to know Aiden for even this short time she would be shocked if he was actually guilty of the crime he was accused of. The police should still be out looking for the real killer. Pax interrupted her train of thought reminding her that he was still here and was her ride home.

"Hey, since we are already in town, let's go by my house and grab some lunch," Pax suggested.

"I guess that would be good. Maybe we can brainstorm over lunch if there is anything that we can do to help Aiden. I feel sort of bad just leaving him here." Luna had no better lunch options and she was not ready to head home.

"We don't really have another option besides leaving him here, he's locked up. We need to let law enforcement do their jobs. We have no idea what the guy is capable of." Pax knew Luna was a softy, but he didn't want her to get taken in by Aiden Birdwhistle's charms.

"Can you actually say that you believe Aiden stabbed or bludgeoned Mayer Dankworth to death? I'm pretty sure there was no mention of a gun being involved. Does he really seem at all violent to you? He followed my dog to make sure Sherlock was okay for heaven's sakes."

"So, he says. I don't know what to think, but let's get out of this place." Pax didn't want to remain anywhere near the proximity of Birdwhistle guilty or not.

The police station was located near the center of town and the university overlooked the city from its east side slopes. They drove in the opposite direction to the west side of town into a densely populated residential area where the Loughty's lived. A park across the street from Pax's house allowed for a feeling of openness even with the other homes so near in proximity preventing Luna from feeling claustrophobic in suburbia.

Helene Loughty greeted Luna warmly as she entered. Pax's mother always made her feel welcome. Pax had offered more than once to let Luna live with him and his mother, but something about the arrangement felt odd. It was better to keep the Loughty home as a backup when needed. Like going home for Thanksgiving or Christmas. She rarely spent holidays with her parents, so this home was that place for her. They were family.

"Hey, mom, mind if we grab a bite." Pax asked.

"There are leftovers from last night's meatloaf or sandwich fixings in the fridge. But the both of you look like your dog just died. Maybe a chocolate sundae is more in order." Helene smiled. Luna was not sure if Mrs. Loughty was joking or not, but the dog dying thing hit a little too close to home. Each person had their own sense of humor she supposed.

"Yeah mom, we just dropped a man off at the police station who is suspected of murder, so things have been a bit heavy, but we're good. Aren't we?"

Luna nodded her head but was not so sure.

"Are you talking about that Birdwhistle fella? Such a shame. He seems like a nice young man." Helene cooed.

What was it about Birdwhistle and women? The guy had even charmed his mother.

"Well, how many killers really seem like killers? I guess a person never knows what's inside a guy." Pax tsked.

"I agree with your mom. Maybe we should have done more for him? Now I feel awful about taking him to the police. We should have kept him at the treehouse until they found the real culprit."

It was time to change the subject. "Meatloaf or black forest ham and cheese?" Pax asked his date. Not that his date considered it a date, but he would take what he could get.

"Oooo, both sound delicious, how about a meatloaf sandwich? Could you toast the bread and cut the meatloaf thin with ketchup? No need to warm it up." Luna requested.

"One meatloaf special coming up." Pax disappeared into the kitchen to fulfill the role of lunchtime chef. Even though he lived at home his mother didn't wait on him at thirty.

Luna was left out in the living room with Helene. The room was clean and comfortable although dated and worn. The décor looked like it had not been updated since Pax was born but there was not one speck of dust on anything. On the wall opposite a picture window embraced by maroon drapes that were drawn back to overlook the park was a wall of photos documenting the lives of the people who lived here or had lived here. A large professional family photo of four was at the center of the collage. Pax's dad Marvin had been gone for almost twenty years and his older sister for probably fifteen. Paisley had not died but was living across the country somewhere with her own growing family of five. The Tumbler family photo was kitty-corner across the room on a bookcase. Marvin was buried in the Moonburg cemetery. Luna had visited his grave with Pax a few times. She could see some of Pax in his father's features especially through the eyes.

Surrounding the classic family portrait were various pictures captured throughout the years. There was grade school Pax in his boy scout uniform and high school Pax with a group of football buddies still in pads and helmets after a championship game. A photo of his college graduation showed Pax in a cap and gown with his arm around Helene's shoulders. Luna thought she may have captured that image. There were just two of the four original family members living here in this home by that time. The pride on his mother's face was palpable. The mother and son really had been a good team over the years.

The idea of accepting Pax's offer to move in and share this home with him and his mother made Luna feel like the third wheel. There was no picture of her on this wall. In some ways it would have been much easier to acquiesce and bundle up all of her belongings to throw in with theirs, but what would her identity be in the threesome. Would she move into Paisley's vacant bedroom as an adopted little sister or was there a romantic possibility between the two of them…she and Pax obviously not with his mother. The man was hard to read. She did think she detected a tad of jealousy from Pax when Aiden was around. But not enough to clarify where his feelings stood. She knew he loved her, but she did not want to be lumped into the same love category as the others in this home. So, moving in had never felt quite right. Besides, where would she gather and dry the ingredients for her herbal teas. She enjoyed her business and had no intention of giving it up. Living near her inventory and available resources was convenient.

Luna could smell the bread toasting. Pax was a good guy, but was he her guy? It was not easy running into appropriate male options in her sequestered world. But she was fine in her world, single or as a couple. Light coming through the window glared off of unidentified metal bling on the bookcase holding Paisley's family photo. Luna glanced over to see a few books mingled between Pax's motocross and wrestling trophies on full display reflecting the light. He was one active rough and tough guy's kind of guy. She knew she was lucky to have him in any compacity in her life and wondered if it was hard for him to be corralled in an office eight hours a day. There likely weren't any trophies for best bank analyst. She supposed that was why Pax had taken a side job for the local newspaper in the sport's department as a part-time reporter writing up sporting events. The journalistic experience allowed him to still keep his finger on the pulse of the action. Perhaps it also gave him an excuse to go to games alone since she was usually not in town during the week to accompany him and most of his buddies from school were married with families of their own these days.

Helene had noticed Luna surveying her humble home and spoke up in a cheery voice, "I know it's not much, but it's home. Have a seat on the sofa or we can sit around the dining table."

"No, your home is a lovely tribute to your family, Helene. I was just thinking about other things. My home growing up was not nearly as warm and homey. I like it here." Luna did not want to make the woman feel inadequate. Who was she to judge homemaking skills? She lived in a tree. Perhaps she should invite Helene to dinner at her place sometime. Luna would guess the woman rarely had a social invitation.

"You know there is always room for one more here if it gets too difficult for you out there alone." Luna could hear the sincerity in the older woman's voice.

Maybe that was it. It was nice having a mother, but Luna didn't want to be mothered really. She liked her independence and her unique living arrangement suited her. "Thanks for the generous offer Mrs. Loughty, that's very gracious of you, but I'm doing well for now."

Pax reappeared with meatloaf sandwiches, chips, and a wedge of dill pickle on two plates, "I thought I would try your newfangled meatloaf sandwich idea too. Didn't want to be coveting your food with a traditional ham and cheese in front of me." Helene faded away as Pax replaced her beside Luna. He was not what one would call classically handsome, more ruggedly good-looking, tall with broad shoulders and unmanageable wavy brown hair that would never stay in place. His hazel eyes always looked at her with warmth and a full-toothed smile exposing a slight space between his two front teeth spread across his face. Luna could imagine worse things than being wrapped in his arms. Her life was complicated. Instead of mentioning their unconventional relationship that she had been pondering, Luna decided to discuss a more manageable topic.

"Okay, so do you think there is anything we can do to help Aiden?"

Disappointment spread across Pax's face, even his culinary attempt had not dissuaded her from the subject of the other man. "I'm not sure what we can do for him. He is locked up behind bars for now and breaking him out doesn't sound like a wise plan. Is there something you'd like me to do that isn't against the law?"

"Funny Pax, I'm sure we can come up with a better option than a jailbreak. There has to be something we can do. This sandwich is delicious by the way." Luna answered through her mouthful.

One win for the meatloaf sandwich. Pax would take it. He knew he was awkward and tried too hard around women, especially Luna. He was not a natural and probably came across weirdly jealous or possessive which was not attractive in any man, and he was not a guy that any woman would swoon over even if he did exude confidence. He just needed this one woman, the one that he was crazy about to see possibilities in him. But dang, she was right, either way, the sandwich was awfully good.

Chapter 7

The Sun travels at 220 kilometers per second. It is 24,000-26,000 light-years from the galaxy center and takes approximately 225-250 million years to complete an orbit of the center of the Milky Way. So far, the Sun has circled the Milky Way 18 times over its lifetime. Different parts of the Sun rotate at different speeds. You can see how fast the surface is rotating by tracking the movement of sunspots across the surface. Regions at the equator take 25 days to complete one rotation, while features at the poles can take 36 days. And the inside of the Sun seems to take about 27 days.

Zori

It was all over the news. Mayor Dankworth's suspected killer had turned himself in. Aiden Birdwhistle was in jail awaiting his arraignment hearing. At future court proceedings, which would hopefully take place over the next few weeks, the criminal defendant would be formally advised of the charges against him and asked to enter a plea. The ongoing debate between newscasters centered around if Mr. Birdwhistle would plead innocent or guilty to his charges.

For some strange, not totally morbid nor fire-truck-chaser reason, Zori was very curious to see the man in jail. Why did he turn himself in? Mr. Birdwhistle might have been able to avoid capture if he was resourceful. What possessed him? Perhaps knowing he was innocent gave him an illusion that the facts would be uncovered, and he would be freed? Didn't he know the justice system was not always just? Sometimes a person had to take things into their own hands for the good of all or at least the good of the accused in this case.

Zori didn't have a car or at least her own specific car. One could reason she actually had hundreds of cars or access to them anyway because her dad said she could drive any car on the lot. She did have a driver's license. Her family was in the car business after all and she was not completely inept. She would pick out a vehicle that didn't stand out on the road and was not easy to identify or remember. It would not do for anyone to know she was visiting a suspected murderer. Although she might be living closer to one than anyone imagined.

A thought percolated in her brain that she could bake the inmate a cake and drop it off on her way to class. A cake delivery would give her a valid reason to visit. Entrance to awkward places was often easier when bearing food. Not too big of a cake, he may not have cellmates to share it with and the jailers might not be allowed to accept a portion of an inmate's food. What kind of cake would do for incarceration? Zori was not aware of a manual outlining appropriate confectionaries for such a situation. She googled *best cakes for a person in jail* and was surprised to see several ideas pop up on her phone screen. There was a recipe for a Jailhouse Cake also known as an Oat Cake which may be tasty but looked too drab and boring. She found an interesting link from an undercover inmate on how to make a cake in prison. The Correctional Cake consisted of Oreo cookies, M&M's, and peanut butter. With no real cooking utensils, they had to use things like trash bags and sharpened spoon handles. The inmate's resourcefulness was impressive. Sugar was certainly a motivator.

Zori eventually clicked on the link *7 Best Jail Cake ideas*. The bakers were obviously making a stab at humor, but she was not sure their goal was accomplished. There was one cake with bright orange pajama-like attire on the top emblazoned with the inmate's actual name. Another with a large black ball connected to an open cuffed chain sporting the frosting words "no more jail." A couple of cakemakers had creatively carved an actual jail cell down into the cake, one decorated with frosting bars another with a complete set of furnishings, well the bed, sink, and toilet.

The most appropriately themed cakes displayed birds flying out from behind the bars of a cage. One airborne bluebird was even wearing a little black and white striped jail uniform. These must be for welcoming home a freed prisoner and that was not the case here, not yet anyway. She could work with a free bird idea but skip the bars and perhaps add song notes instead. Yes, that would represent 'bird whistle' nicely while not drawing reference to his incarceration. The flavor did not matter so much since she did not know his favorite. Zori would go with the basic chocolate or white and maybe dye the batter blue to match what he must be feeling. She would get right on it, having a purpose to focus on made her feel better.

The cake began to take shape. Baking was therapeutic. While the layers cooled enough for her to add the frosting, Zori decided to call her mother and check in. She wanted to ask someone she trusted about her jail-visit idea, and she was not comfortable asking her dad. He would definitely say no.

Zori dialed the memorized number that she had punched into her phone too many times to count over the years. Her mother's upbeat recorded voice rang in her ears,

"So sorry I cannot pick up right now, I would hate to miss anything you have to say, so please leave a message." Once again Zori was not going to be able to speak with her mom so left a message as instructed.

"Hey mom, I really need to talk when you have a minute. There's a lot going on here these days. The Mayor was murdered. He may have deserved it, but it is still sad. I think I am going to take a cake to the guy in jail who the police think did it. Just wondered if you thought that was okay. Miss you. This is Zori again." She hung up the phone. Maybe her mom had forgotten her.

###############################

Zori gave herself an extra thirty minutes to stop at the jail. She probably only needed five to leave the cake and maybe take a peek at the prisoner, but she didn't want to be late for class in case things didn't go as planned. Her weekly class was on Wednesdays, but Zori hadn't been able to wait until then. She felt restless and nearly possessed to see the man accused of the crime. Their Baking 201 instructor had invited a guest lecturer to speak to those interested in catering tonight at the college. Those who attended could earn extra credit. She hadn't been sure she wanted to attend the presentation, she was getting an A anyway, until the idea to visit the recently arrested gentleman on the way came into her mind.

The officer in charge ogled her bird-with-song-notes cake before offering to let her go back and deliver it to the prisoner in person. Mr. Birdwhistle must not be deemed too dangerous. Zori's curiosity urged her on and she entered through the locked door into the underbelly of the police station holding the cake before her like a shield to ward off dark forces.

Aiden Birdwhistle sat dejectedly on a bare cot. He did not look threatening even with his muscular build. Haggard eyes appearing to be blue stared off into space. His sandy blonde hair was discolored by some hair product that made the front section above his forehead stand on end. Even disheveled from a night in jail his cleft-chinned face was attractive. Her coloring was similar to the convicts, with some of its intensity leaked out. Her hair was a whiter blonde, not so sandy, and her eyes were a paler blue similar to the color created if both the inside and outside of the robin's eggshell were mixed. She was a female version of this man without the depth of hues.

Aiden acknowledged her presence by rising to stand. He was taller than she was, medium height for a man, but his physic was more fit. Zori was not what an observer would consider overweight, perhaps a little pudgy from ingesting one too many baked treats.

"An angel bearing gifts, is that delicacy for me? What's the occasion?" Aiden flashed her a tired smile. "You mustn't have liked the Mayor too well if the cake is any indication. I cannot imagine what you would have brought if I had done something truly heroic. Hope you thought to bake a file into it," Aiden teased. Zori was surprised that the man in front of her could still be jovial under the circumstances and could sense skepticism of her motives behind his humor.

She wasn't shy, more uncomfortable, and not sure how to explain her odd offering. "I'm just sorry that you're behind bars and hoped a cake might cheer you up." Sheesh, she sounded like the president of his fan club. Zori knew there were women who were attracted to imprisoned men. He probably thought she was one of those wackos.

"It isn't your fault my nameless, cake-bearing friend. Hopefully, they find the right guy before too long. I didn't do it you know. I'm sure all prisoners say that, but I didn't."

"Zori, I'm Zori and I believe you." Her dad would be ultra-angry that she came if he knew. He would not want her to draw any negative attention in his direction. She would be very careful to not let Marcus MacQuiod, the more likely killer of the two, find out. Not wanting to leave just yet, but having no reason to be there or stay she unexpectedly added, "Can I visit you again?"

"As you can see my social calendar is pretty open." Aiden jested.

"Any requests for next time? Foodwise that is, I enjoy baking. I'm in a class at the college." Like he cared. Zori realized that this whole visiting Aiden thing was slightly insane, but she couldn't help herself, and baked condolences were a nice buffer.

"If you're serious and it isn't an imposition, carrot cake or oatmeal raisin cookies are my favorites, that is only if you really don't mind."

It would give her an excuse to come again. "Then I'll bring one of those two selections you've ordered on each of my next two visits."

"I'm hoping not to be here that long, but it will give me something to look forward to. Thanks."

The jailer reappeared to escort Zori out. But first, the guard unlocked and opened the cell door enough to allow the cake to fit through. She had forgotten a serving plate and utensils. Darn it. Did she expect the prisoner to eat the cake with his hands like a barbarian? What an insult.

"Um, I forgot a plate and fork. If you could bring them with his next meal, I would appreciate it." Zori asked the accommodating officer before rushing off to Baking 201.

Her phone buzzed with an incoming text as she climbed into the nondescript white Ford with MacQuiod Motors temporary license plates. Unfortunately, it was not her mother on the other end of the cyber connection but her father wanting to "have a talk" with her when she got home. He even spelled out her full name, Zoriah. That could not be good. Zori was awkward around her father and suddenly afraid he must have found out somehow that she had dropped by the jail before class. How could he have known so fast? She was still sitting in the jail parking lot. Did he have spies or a GPS tracker on her? She hated that she felt it should be her father behind bars instead of Aiden. What a terrible daughter she was. He was her dad and the only family member she really had left in her life; she could never abandon or betray him.

Before putting away her phone to allow for undistracted driving Zori quickly responded, "C U @ 10." Giving herself plenty of time to drive the hour home after the class lecturer. She should have snagged a slice of her comfort food, the jailbird cake, to snack on during the stressful drive home. What did her father want with her anyway? Her plate was becoming more cluttered than she liked despite giving a fully loaded one away today with the cake on it. She did not even have an extra plate to serve a slice from. Zori chuckled to herself at her mental plate-puns. She would take one day at a time, breathe, and see where she ended up. She pulled into the Moonbeam University parking lot already looking forward to her next visit with the incarcerated Aiden Birdwhistle.

Chapter 8

The distance between the Sun and the Earth changes throughout the year. This is because the Earth travels in an elliptical orbit around the Sun. The distance between the two bodies varies from 147 to 152 million kilometers. The distance between the Earth and the Sun is measured as an Astronomical Unit (AU).

Aiden

Aiden's family finally made it down to the jail in Moonburg to visit him. His hometown was only an hour away and it had taken them over twenty-four hours since he was booked and placed behind bars to get there. That was on top of the twenty-four plus hours that he had been in the woods. Their lack of devotion was less than touching. Besides the cake girl and a stream of guards bringing bad meals on a regular basis, Aiden had mostly been in isolation. The Mooonburg jail was not packed with prisoners which for the most part was a good thing. He had heard stories of what happened to younger men behind bars and was not hoping to act out that scenario. A surly guard who was either putting on a tough guy show for the family or had missed his morning coffee, led Aiden to a larger room to accommodate the family visit.

His parents insisted that they had been working on their son's behalf from behind the scenes and his mother had been too upset until now to see her son locked up. Her blotchy face with bloodshot red eyes was an obvious reminder of how his situation had affected his mom. It had taken a full day for her to regain and maybe even maintain her composure after hearing the dreadful news. Aiden was not surprised that the woman who would not even allow a swear word in her midst could not bear to see her son in such degradation. However, it was not as if he was imprisoned in the Big House with hardened criminals. Aiden would be surprised if they housed more than unruly drunks and traffic offenders in this jail.

Rocco came along on the family visit in apparent chipper spirits countering his mother's gloom. The whole thing appeared to be a romp for him. His teenaged brother found it beyond cool to have a notorious sibling who in his testosterone addled mind "added street cred with the chicks by having spent time in the pen".

"You've got to be kidding me," was the only response Aiden gave to his brother's dumb comment. "What if I never get out!"

Aiden's dad holding the middle ground with his emotions flatly informed, "The police have no other leads at this time son and the court considers you a flight risk since you've already fled the scene once, so no bail has been set."

The news was not hopeful. To add to the blow, his parents sadly confessed that they didn't have the financial means to provide a top-notch lawyer or they would lose their business. Aiden was going to be stuck with his uncle, his mom's younger brother Tobias Berrycloth who had never won a case in his career and had never represented anyone being tried for murder before. The unfortunate news just kept rolling in.

"Don't worry Aiden, Toby will take care good of you, your family," his mother sounded more optimistic than any of them felt. They all knew Uncle Toby was definitely something to worrying about.

A few hours later, Aiden watched this same uncle saunter into the holding cell where they were allowed to meet to discuss his case. Uncle Toby's suit was not expensively tailored. It was tight in places where it would look better loose and loose in places it should be tight. He was wearing a white shirt and tie, well sort of white and quite wrinkled with the pink patterned tie askew and off to the side. His uncle's appearance did not ooze confidence into the accused man confined behind bars. Uncle Toby was his mother's little brother, but closer to his age than hers. Toby had been born later in Aiden's grandparent's lives and never really grown up as far as Aiden could tell. Aiden had always felt like he was older than his uncle or at least more mature.

Toby's hair was not cut any better than his suit and the hair product he used left white flakes that resembled dandruff across his disheveled head of dark hair. Maybe the man was merely going prematurely gray and that effect created the illusion of the lighter flecks, but it didn't look as if they were attached. On the opposite end of his head, his uncle either needed a shave or was going for the stubble look and not pulling it off well. In the middle of his face puffy dark skin bagged under dull gray eyes whether, from lack of sleep due to hard work on a case or a late night of heavy drinking, Aiden was not sure which. Not that Aiden looked spiffy himself, but he had an excuse. This place was not exactly a spa.

It was family knowledge that Tobias Berrycloth had never been what one would call a good student, but supposedly his uncle had watched various legal shows on TV while growing up and decided the lifestyle of an attorney was the way to go as a career track. By some miracle of fate or affirmative action clause that Aiden was not aware of, Tobias Berrycloth been accepted into the local law school after college. Toby's ancient grandfather was an alma mater of the institution and according to Aiden's mother, that fact alone pulled some strings for his only grandson. It took Tobias three attempts at the state bar exam to finally pass. This uncle on the Berrycloth side passed with the minimum score needed and begun his fledgling career with his own office since no other firms had hired him.

Uncle Toby did pro bono work to gain experience and had actually only snagged a few paying cases that Aiden was aware of. The clients that Tobias defended were all guilty according to Toby, so he felt it was not really his fault that he had not been able to get them off the hook. From his uncle's point of view, at least he had tried on their behalf. Hopefully, things would go better when he was representing his own nephew. This was going to be a high-profile case so it would give *Berrycloth Attorney at Law* free advertising however it turned out. Aiden was hoping not to be another tally mark on the loss column of his uncle's unimpressive career. The man was long overdue for a win.

"Hello Nephew," Tobias stretched out his hand to shake Aiden's, "sorry we aren't meeting under better circumstances. Hopefully, we will have you home for family Thanksgiving dinner."

Was the man joking or did he really believe that was possible? "Thanks for your help, Uncle Toby. I didn't do it, so I sure hope so."

"Of course not, just keep telling me that. And I don't want to know otherwise if you did," Tobias smiled. Not even his teeth looked tidy.

"No, I *really* didn't do it. I'm innocent. I just need for *you* to prove that" Aiden insisted.

"Keep telling me that. But the evidence may prove otherwise. The investigators don't seem to be able to find any indication or evidence of anyone else at the scene of the crime. Have you considered a possible plea bargain? Say manslaughter? Your parents said that your family was pretty upset with the new tariffs on the business. Perhaps you two were just arguing and things got out of hand? Or you just flipped out?"

Really? Was the man kidding or merely an idiot? "Uncle…"

"You can call me Tobias or Mr. Berrycloth. We should probably keep things more professional; it'll be good practice for when we're in court."

"How many times do I have to tell you. I DIDN'T DO IT! I don't even know how the mayor was killed. I just found him unconscious and bleeding all over his beige carpet with no pulse. I AM INNOCENT!" Aiden was getting frustrated. His uncle, Aiden refused to call him Mr. Berrycloth, was not even listening to him.

"So, you're telling me you don't want to plead guilty to a lesser crime? They have you on first-degree murder charges right now and the sentencing, if they convict you of that crime will not be pretty. Not sure you want to test your luck with than one, Mr. Birdwhistle. I could get you off with eight to twenty years for manslaughter, less if I could convince them it was involuntary. And you'd be out much earlier than you're actually sentenced with good behavior. If you're convicted of first-degree murder you could get hammered with twenty to life or worse." His uncle drew his thumb across his neck like he was slitting his own throat. How encouraging.

Uncle Toby had moved the conversation between the two of them to a more formal place avoiding any terms of intimacy, had Aiden somehow missed the 'you are family' vibe that his mom was talking about? The man was not only an incompetent moron, he was also a jerk. Fine, they did not have to use familial terms, but Aiden refused to give the guy the respect of being addressed as a professional.

"I'm telling you *Toby*; I refuse to plead guilty to something *I did not do*. A plea bargain indicates that I agree that I did kill the mayor, which I didn't, either by accident or on purpose." Aiden was getting exasperated. "You can at least tell me how the man died and perhaps share some other options that we can both agree on. Pleading guilty is out."

"Okay, I'll let you sleep on that decision to make sure you understand the gravity of the situation," Uncle Toby was pulling out all of his big words now. The man probably feared his lack of ability to get Aiden off and wanted to save his nephew's neck for his big sister's sake. "And the police don't have the weapon in their possession at this time, but it is believed Mayor Dankworth was stabbed more than once with a sharp object. Only one of the blows was lethal. It penetrated his carotid artery. Accounting for the large pool of blood you saw sopped up by the carpet. If you know where the weapon might be that could help our plea."

Help how? His uncle obviously did not believe his innocence. "Great, give me until tomorrow. I won't change my mind about being guilty, but maybe I can think of something else." His lawyer certainly wasn't being open-minded to any other options. 'You get what you pay for' appeared to be true in this case. His parents were going bargain-basement shopping with his life.

Uncle Toby left sucking all the air out of the room with him. Aiden felt a shroud of doom envelop him. There had to be a better option even if he was stuck dealing with incompetence.

"You have other visitors waiting to see you, can I bring them in now before I take you back to the cell?" The guard asked.

Wow, his third group of company or gathering of sightseers in a single day, Aiden's social life seemed to be picking up in his pre-prison world. "Why not, bring 'em in." This visit certainly couldn't be worse than the last.

Luna with the Paxman shadowing her were led into the room. The big guy's body language telegraphed that he didn't want to be there. Did Pax think his woman needed a bodyguard for safety in Aiden's presence even when he was incarcerated, or could he actually be jealous of an imagined connection between the two of them? Luna was a sharp woman, and the age difference didn't bother Aiden, but really, what kind of move could he make on her in jail? Pax definitely overestimated his skills with women, and it was absurd to think this place conducive for conjugal visits.

"I just wanted to check in on you and see how you're doing. I feel it's partly our fault since we're the ones who brought you here," Luna seemed sincerely sorry.

"I've been better, but it's not your fault. Just please believe I'm innocent." Aiden requested.

"Of course, that was never a question. I know you didn't do it." Luna responded immediately, but Pax still didn't look so sure.

"Well, that makes one of you. Even my lawyer doesn't seem convinced and he is related," Aiden dejectedly admitted. "Looks like I'm going to be stuck here for a while."

"We'll do what we can and look around, to see if we can find out anything if that helps. Won't we Pax?" Luna prodded.

Pax spoke up for the first time, "Sure, I'll help Luna or at least be her driver if she wants me to."

"That'd be great. I'm sort of indisposed at the moment and no one seems to be looking for anyone else who might have committed the crime or even had a motive. They've decided that they already have their man and unfortunately that man is me," Aiden confessed. With a dog named Sherlock, these two were bound to be decent detectives, weren't they? He would have to take his chances with an ineffective family barrister and amateur friend sleuths. Yikes. Aiden was a pretty positive guy by nature, but his hope was being stretched precariously thin. It was going to take superhuman efforts to vault over this teetering crossbar.

Chapter 9

The temperature inside of the Sun can reach 15 million degrees Celsius. Energy is generated at the Sun's core, by nuclear fusion, as hydrogen converts to helium. Hot objects expand, so the Sun would explode if it were not for its enormous gravitational force. The temperature on the surface of the Sun is close to 5,600 degrees Celsius. The Sun is slowly heating up and becoming 10% more luminous every billion years. Within a billion years, the heat from the Sun will be so intense that some scientists believe liquid water won't exist on the surface of the Earth. Every second the Sun emits more energy than humans have used in the last 10,000 years. And every day, plants convert sunlight into energy, consuming the equivalent of six times the power that has been used in all human history.

Luna

A chaplain crossed paths with Luna and Pax as they exited the jail. It was Sunday and the man of the cloth was likely visiting the less fortunate here behind bars. Her parents had never taken Luna to church while growing up, but she believed there was a higher power or a supreme being of some sort doling out karma to those here on earth. Everything that surrounded her was too perfect and symbiotic to have just happened. Her very being told her that there was more than what met the eye in this existence. Luna hoped the holy man was going to stop in and visit Aiden to disperse some of his understanding and perhaps give comfort.

The sun was dropping behind the mountain and it would soon be totally dark. As they climbed into his SUV Pax suggested, "Hey, it is getting late. I hate to drop you off in pitch blackness. You're welcome to stay over. I have work in the morning, but you could drop me off and start some of your undercover sleuthing if you'd like. Then I'd take you back to the treehouse after work?"

"I'm sure your mother would just love having me for a sleepover, however, I forgot to bring my footsy jammies," Luna quipped a tad sarcastically.

"You know my mom loves you and I've never pegged you for a girl who had any issues with roughing it," Pax countered.

"Even though the offer is tempting, I left Sherlock home alone. He'd probably be fine, but I'd feel awful if he took off looking for me and got lost. He was almost got hit by a car the other day, or I guess it was a truck, remember. That's how all this got started." Luna had mixed emotions about staying overnight at Pax's house. Going home was for the best.

"Heck, I even lose out to dogs these days. Alright, I'll take you back to the hairy male of your choice. Maybe I need to grow a beard." Luna thought she detected both humor and a touch of hurt in Pax's voice. "Next time let's bring Sherlock with us. My mom likes dogs, we can leave him with her while we do whatever we need to do on your save-Aiden mission. Wait, that guy lowers me down to at least third on your list of favorite males."

"Yeah, yeah, funny. How about next Saturday when you come, we can take a trip to Starville and have a look around?" Luna suggested, "And I'll take a raincheck on the sleepover."

"You actually think we'll be able to find anything that the professionals didn't?" Pax was skeptical.

"We look unassuming enough, just a goofy girl and teddy bear of a guy, so people won't be on their guard around us. We can go on a fake date to a coffee shop or bar in the area and see what the locals are saying about things. It could be fun." Luna perked up.

"First of all, 'teddy bear of a guy' comment stabs me in the heart, ouch. Not exactly the description a man likes to hear about himself. And you give off more of a Pippy Longstockings vibe with your thick reddish locks, especially when they're braided, and with your freckle-spattered nose, definitely not goofy. Give us both more credit. We'd make a dashing couple, so why does the date have to be fake?"

Pax was fun to be with. "Okay, we can be a detective duo, partners in uncovering crime. The date can be an extension of our team efforts, not fake. Does that make it better?" Luna didn't want to offend her best human friend.

"I'll take what I can get and plan to come up earlier than usual on Saturday to give us more time. Bring the beast if you want to stay over, if not I'll bring you back before too late. Honestly though, what makes you think we can make a difference?"

"I don't know. But I'd at least like to give it a try. You have journalistic skills that might be able to uncover more than you think you can," Luna bolstered their efforts.

"My journalistic skills are definitely in a very narrow arena. If the killer dropped a pass and we find the ball near the scene of the crime or a cleat from his shoe was left behind as he ran away, we may have something." Pax was more comfortable deflecting his inadequacies with humor. "You do know that I cover sport's stories, right?"

"Well, you never know when we might score a touchdown or sink a long shot basket or even hit a home run," Luna continued with his imagery, "but I think we will make a good team and I have a gut feeling the authorities are missing something."

"Okay, I'll play on your team until I'm traded," Pax gave in.

The two pulled up in front of the treehouse, headlights from the vehicle shining into Sherlock's golden eyes. The dog was waiting for his beloved Luna and rushed the car as she climbed out covering her with kisses as he did a hind-legged dance around her feet.

"How can I compete with love like that?" Pax chuckled.

Luna thought of inviting Pax to come in. Her place loomed before her in the darkness. Having his company might be nice tonight. Maybe just for a mug of tea. But having him stay over at her place would be even more awkward than her staying at his. With only two tiny rooms where would he sleep? On her table? She was not ready to think about the other options.

Instead, she spoke, "Thanks for the ride into town two days in a row. That was above and beyond. You're awesome as always. See you on Saturday. Say nine-thirty-ish?" Luna saw the hopeful humor dim from Pax's eyes even in the darkness.

"Sure, see you then. I'll just wait here until you get inside so my headlights can shine some light for you until you enter." Pax always the gentleman, but never quite ready to make his move offered. Luna led by Sherlock who romped up the ramp, unlocked her narrow wooden door, then waved goodbye before disappearing inside and shutting it behind them. She watched the headlights drive away as she turned on an electric lantern that warmed the cozy room with its soft glow. Was it weird she was content to sleep next to her dog? Pax was equally loyal and had other perks to offer. The thought made her fair skin blush. Avoiding the bedroom, Luna climbed the ladder to her loft.

If the people in Moonburg thought that she was strange in high school and college, they should take a peek at her budding business draped all around her now. Drying herbs and fruits dangled from strings strung across the lower edge of the peaked ceiling where it met the wall creating a fringed triangle. As long as an ingredient wasn't poisonous and could be dried to make tea leaves, Luna was willing to try about any flavor combination. Mint leaves, ginger roots, and cinnamon bark hung next to wild strawberry plants, varieties of blackberries, and blossom honey. She used whatever she could scrounge, pine needles, dandelion leaves, even dried moss which had not been too tasty. Some combos were even medicinal. Slippery elm and licorice leaves soothed the throat. What did she feel like tonight? Chamomile sounded nice for sleep with pineapple weed for a kick of flavor.

Her former critics and tormentors may find her attic loft more befitting a witch coven's den to brew up spells in a caldron than see it for what it really was...an impressive collection from nature to use for the healing arts. Luna was not planning to be burned at the stake any time in the near future. Her tea business was growing and becoming legit. The world was going gaga for the weak substance and she was in on the ground floor, or perhaps on the tip-top of the movement was a more appropriate analogy. Not that tea hadn't been around forever, but it was having a resurgence.

The most popular origin story of the warm liquid that she could find traced back five thousand years when supposedly camellia leaves drifted into a cup of hot water being drunk by Shennong, the Emperor of China. Other theories pointed to different eras and different accidents of discovery, but scholars generally agreed that southwest China is where it originated. Wherever it began, the popularity of tea was undeniable. It had become the most consumed beverage in the world outside of water, beloved for its taste, health benefits, and the way it brought people together.

Luna originally played off of her last name and called her business *Ferns-Bee Teas* with a bumblebee on a fern as the logo. Lately, she was pondering changing it to *Treehouse Teas*. Now would be the time, before it got too much bigger. She could still handle the operation by herself printing off and cutting out the cute logos, then filling premade tea bags with one tablespoon blends of dried leaf combinations. Heat-sealed tea bags would have worked well, but in her environment, it was easier to simply staple the bags shut with a six-inch string knotted on each end, then connect the logo label to the individual tea bags with another staple. Hand-written stickers revealing the flavor contained were stuck to the backside of the logo tags. Lastly, the small fiber teas bags were grouped in numbers of ten and boxed to sell.

It was a low-budget business at this point all under Luna's own roof. She sold to local markets and mailed out to a few other establishments around the state. Once her distribution grew outside this area, she may need to reconsider her manufacturing plan. Perhaps she never wanted it to grow big enough that she couldn't handle it all herself. There was something satisfying about having a one hundred percent hands-on business.

At the bottom of the ladder, Sherlock started to whine for her attention. Her tea loft was the one spot he had not figured out how to breach which was beneficial in keeping her product clean from outside contaminates. It was time to spend some time with the official male figure in her life. Luna had been absent a lot over the last few days. She shinnied down the ladder and let her dog embrace her with nuzzles. His presence was comforting and did keep her warm at night. Things could be worse in the companion department.

"What kind of tea would you like in your bowl tonight Sherlock?" Luna asked as she scratched a sweet spot behind his ears, she didn't want to leave her dog without a treat tonight too. "Perhaps I'll stir in a spoonful of peanut butter for sweetener. You'd like that."

Luna sipped her tea wondering if Pax and Aiden were each receiving some kind of refreshment tonight to make them both feel better. She sure hoped so.

Chapter 10

__The Sun has a very strong magnetic field.__ Magnetic energy released by the Sun during magnetic storms causes solar flares that appear as sunspots. In sunspots, the magnetic lines twist and spin, much like a tornado would on Earth. The gravity of the Sun anchors the Earth and all the other planets together in the Solar System. Without the Sun, the Earth would travel in a straight line and there would be no life on Earth. The Sun produces energy that supports all life from its warmth and as well as a process known as photosynthesis.

Zori

Zori's dad usually met with her at the dealership for any communication needed since he spent the vast majority of his time there. It felt odd having a chat in the intimacy of their own home. Her father generally reserved home for sleeping, an occasional late-night meeting, or a rare social event. But here he was, bigger than life, Marcus MacQuiod, sitting on a bar stool as she entered the kitchen. The smell of cigars lingered in the air although the man didn't smoke in front of her. Did he think she didn't know? Or was he trying to spare her from lung cancer?

"I'm glad you made it home, honey. Off doing more school or something fun for once on a Saturday night?" Zori doubted he really cared where she was. Daddy Marcus was probably just schmoozing and softening her up before dropping whatever bomb he had on her.

"Both…school can be fun, dad. It isn't all budgeting classes." She would give him the benefit of the doubt, maybe he was more interested in her life than she imagined. "I was at a catering lecture."

"Well, hopefully, they at least fed you a good meal for attending," he acknowledged.

"There were a few appetizers so I'm not hungry now. Since you wanted to talk, I hurried home." She hadn't really hurried home, but maybe her tilted perspective would help him get to the point.

"You trust me don't you, Zoriah?" He refrained from looking her into the eyes as he asked.

Zori wanted to answer his question honestly but carefully, "I'm trying to."

"What kind of answer is that?" Her dad huffed, "I know you may have been exposed to some things at work that might look questionable, but I'm always there for you, baby girl."

The semi-sleazy 'baby girl' made Zori throw up a little bit in her mouth, "I know you try to be there, and you do provide well for me, dad. I just miss mom." She did miss her mother immensely and her dad probably did try, but he was somewhat scary. She was not surprised that her mother had left. However, the tone in his next reply was gentler than Zori had heard his voice since she was a little girl.

"I wish Vada was here too. I do miss her."

Zori actually believed that he did, the man sounded sincere, then he continued in a more concerned tone, "You know that we are involved in some business dealings with the mayor. Or were."

"That makes sense, I know Mayor Dankworth was around the dealership regularly, but I don't know many details."

"And you don't need to know the details. I just want to make sure if the police question you that you don't share anything damning or perhaps, I should say damaging instead. Alright?" Marcus MacQuiod patted his adult daughter on the shoulder in confirmation of his request.

"Why would I, dad?" Zori knew why she could but wasn't sure she would.

"I'm not saying you would, sweetheart. It's just that things might have looked different than they really were, and I am just clarifying for you that everything is okay and above board. There's nothing to worry your pretty little head about. In fact, it's probably for the best that you don't even talk with any law enforcement. It might be upsetting for you." Yeah, now Zori was pretty positive that her dad wasn't more worried about her than he was for himself in this situation.

"I'll do my best to keep our family safe," was all Zori replied. "I'm tired tonight, long day, can I go now?"

"Sure, sure, go get some sleep. Sweet dreams dearest daughter."

Zori was almost certain that her dad had used more terms of endearment in this conversation than he had for the last several years combined. She thought she counted at least four or perhaps five. The man was indeed the ultimate salesman. She needed to talk to her mom. Down to earth, common-sense communication would help her get the nauseatingly sticky-sweet taste out of her mouth. Zori pulled out her phone, speed dialed, and started speaking.

"Mom, I miss you so much tonight. Dad and I had a talk. We both miss you. Things would be so much easier if

96

you were here. I'm afraid dad is involved in something not good. Really bad really. I haven't actually seen anything specific. I just have a strong feeling that things aren't okay. I need your advice. Is it the right thing to stick up and cover for family members even if you think they're in the wrong? It's a huge dilemma in my heart. Did you love dad? He must have been a good guy at some point for you to marry him…"

Right in the middle of her soliloquy while pouring out her heart to her mother the call unexpectedly cut out. Was the reception bad wherever her mother happened to be? Had she heard anything that Zori had shared? Would Vada call back with a reply? Zori yearned for the sweet dreams that her father had wished for her but talking with her mother would have been better.

She pulled down the shade and drew the ruffly white drapes across her bedroom window before changing out of her clothes to get ready for bed. Pulling a silky nightgown over her head, she went into the bathroom adjoining her room and splashed water onto her face wiping off the minimal makeup. Then she brushed her teeth avoiding her reflection in the mirror. Perhaps her dad did look out for her and maybe she was a little spoiled. Zori didn't know too many girls who had their own bedroom/bathroom suite when growing up. Of course, by now most girls her age had moved out and had their own apartments with a living room and kitchen too. She had this house pretty much to herself so had never felt the need to leave. Her dad was rarely in her space. Tonight, was the exception.

Strangely enough, as she crawled into bed the person that she most felt like talking to was Aiden Birdwhistle. She imagined the prisoner sleeping on the narrow metal cot with a single blanket and no pillow. Why was she thinking of him? The more she tried not to, the more he came into her mind. She knew she should wait a while before she went to visit Aiden again. What would he think if she came so soon? How long would it take him to finish the jailbird cake that she had baked for him? It didn't matter, she felt utterly compelled to go see him again and couldn't wait a full week. She would force herself to wait until her class on Wednesday if she could make it that long. Going every day would definitely draw attention and create suspicion. But suspicion for what? She didn't know.

Her biggest dilemma was which requested treat to take him? Maybe she would bring both of his requests...a small carrot cake with cream cheese icing and a dozen large soft chewy oatmeal cookies. Sugar made people feel better, it was comforting. What else did he have to spend his time doing in jail? Perhaps he could parlay out any leftover treats to elicit needed favors from the guards. Thoughts of Aiden mixed in with baking filled her dreams. Both topics were indeed sweet, her father's wish for her worked out well.

Zori barely make it all the way until Wednesday for her next visit. Fortunately, things got busy at MacQuoid Motors and she had some additional baking to keep her occupied. The first five minutes of her jailhouse visit with Aiden were extremely awkward. She sat outside the cell across from the bars that divided them on a chair provided for that very purpose. Their conversation was not flowing easily but Zori was not ready to leave even though she could sense the strain in the air was making Aiden increasingly ill at ease. Quiet was okay with her, being near him and occasionally listening was enough for now. Aiden, however, didn't seem as comfortable with the silence and kept making random comments. He probably wondered what in the world she was doing there. Zori wondered what she was doing here as well.

"What do you do when you're not baking cakes for convicts?" Aiden tried to pull her into a conversation.

"I work for my dad at his car dealership and go to college some," Ugh, her life sounded boring. "I know you pole vault?" Zori attempted to keep the conversation going.

"Back in the glory days of my previous life I was a pole vaulter before I sold sunbeams in a box and became incarcerated for murder," he didn't really sound bitter but had more of a flat affect in his voice.

"Was it hard?" She continued.

"Which one, the selling, the murdering, or the vaulting?" There was a twinkle of humor in his voice.

Zori stifled a giggle, "The pole vaulting. It looks so hard."

"There is it, the first smile I have gotten from you in two visits. Your answer is yes, it was challenging but that was part of the joy in it. I competed in other events as well, high jump and some sprints, mostly in the one hundred meters. Poling vaulting combines the need for a sprinter's speed with upper body strength and then you have to use an outside object which you have little control over, the pole, adding to the complication."

"Was it dangerous?"

"At times, especially if you fall wrong. Vaulters have been injured and a few have died. I didn't think about that when competing. I focused on how high I could go. It felt like I was flying when I would plant and push off the pole into the air."

"Why'd you stop?" Zori was becoming a real chatty Cathy.

"For practical reasons, I guess. Realistically, I wasn't going to make the Olympics. The high school pole vault record is just over nineteen feet, ten inches. I was vaulting over sixteen feet regularly which put me with the top vaulters in our state. My record was exactly eighteen feet, but I only hit that height once. I could've gotten a scholarship to college. Maybe not at a school with one of the bigger track and field programs, but..."

"But what?" Zori was truly interested and asked naturally.

"It's water under the bridge as they say. My dad's business was struggling. He needed my help and had plans for me to run it someday. Someday just came earlier than I planned."

"Didn't they want you to go to off college and live your dream?"

"Of course, they would have supported me if that's what I chose. I just realized if I left, there probably wasn't going to be any business to come back to and it's almost impossible to pole vault for a living." Aiden smiled wryly. His answer was spoken matter of fact and solicited no pity.

Zori noticed the time. She was going to be late for her class but didn't care. To change the melancholy topic, she held up the treats she had brought him. "I made them small enough to fit between the bars this time, I think they can anyway. The cake's layers are thin, if we turn it carefully sideways, it should fit, and the cookies will be easy of course." The two exchanged the baked delicacies between themselves without too much trouble, only leaving a smear of frosting across one of the metal bars. "You can save that frosting for later," Zori joked, "What do you want me to bring you next time?"

"Next time? Nothing. You have given me plenty, just the visits are great. As you can see, I can use the company." Then observing the crestfallen look on her face, he quickly added, "Unless food delivery is your ticket into this joint. Then a frosted sugar cookie would be wonderful. Make it two and we can eat them together as we talk."

Sugar cookies were one of Zori's favorites to make and eat. She would roll them out and cut them into a meaningful shape, not yet sure what that shape might be. "Perfect, two sugar cookies coming up next time." She gave Aiden another of her rare smiles. It was sweeter than the cookies.

"Until next time." Aiden smiled back at her with an easy non-forced smile. Were they becoming friends? It felt like they were and that felt nice. What was being thirty minutes late for class among friends she figured.

Chapter 11

One day the Sun will consume the Earth. When the Sun has burned all its hydrogen, it will continue to burn helium for 130 million more years. During this time, it will expand to the point that it will engulf Mercury, Venus, and the Earth. At this stage, it will have become a red giant. After its red giant phase, the Sun will collapse. When this happens, it will become a tiny white dwarf approximately the size of the Earth

Pax

Pax was not sure why he didn't really like the guy. Aiden was a pleasant enough fellow, even behind bars and they had sports in common. Birdwhistle had participated in scholastic sports a few years after Pax had finished his competitive career so they were never direct opponents on any field. And though they played different sports, there was generally a common ground and mutual respect shared among athletes. They all understood the focus and hard work required to compete. Pax was aware of Aiden's success in track and field. Was he jealous? Not of the guy's athletic prowess but maybe of his ability to draw Luna's affection or at least tap into her womanly concern. Would Luna make such an effort to search out things for Pax's own benefit? Possibly, she was that kind of girl.

Standing before him was that kind of girl. Luna got into his car with a smile beaming across her face. She was waiting and ready when he arrived.

"No dog today?" Pax asked.

"Sherlock will be fine here. We'll be less distracted without him and not have to take extra time to detour and drop him off with your mom. I'll bring him next time if we need his bloodhound nose for anything."

"Okay, if you say so, boss." Pax deciphered her dog arrangement to mean that Luna had decided to not stay over tonight. Perhaps he could read clues better than he thought he could. "We're off and on our way to accomplishing mission Spy Date in Starville." His comment made Luna laugh. Pax liked to make her laugh. The light and airy sound floated around him making all feel right in the world.

They didn't have a designated plan as they drove into the area of town where the mayor had been murdered. It was over a week since the dastardly deed had been committed so there was no hoopla still hovering around. This section of the town appeared to be a mix of commercial-type properties, office buildings stood beside what looked like warehouses and a few eating establishments were interspersed throughout. Even a bar appeared to be open barely before noon. The residents in Starville needed to eat and to be able to consume libations at any time of the day it seemed.

"Pick your pleasure, Miss Fernsby. Where would you like to start our spy date?"

"Not that I'm thirsty, but alcohol does loosen the tongue and I'm sure that the Silver Star Bar serves lunch as well. Let's cozy up to some locals in there and see what we can learn. What'd you say, partner?" Luna did not make a convincing cowgirl, but role-playing could be fun. Pax was going to like pretending to be a couple whatever their artificial backgrounds. Heaven knew he could use the practice.

They entered through the grimy weathered-wood door with a rectangle slice of stained glass stretched laterally across the top at eye level adding a touch of church to the experience. The hole-in-the-wall establishment had a few patrons at this hour but was definitely not packed. There was no hostess to greet and seat them, so Pax placed his hand lightly against the small of Luna's back and guided her to a table. A lemony smell from her hair with a hint of some spice that she had likely harvested herself wafted his way. He was smitten and he knew it. Now what to do about it? Helping Luna with her current project was the next best move in his sport's manual brain. And he was hungry.

A server arrived at their table wearing less material across both the top and bottom of her uniform than Pax was accustomed to seeing at the restaurants he generally frequented. The woman, older than a girl, but her age was hard to distinguish in the low light, haphazardly dropped two menus onto their table and asked what she could get them to drink. Pax waited to take Luna's lead before he ordered either a soda or beer.

"Water is good for me right now, thanks." Water might be the most dangerous drink of all in this swampy area, but his pretend date did not seem worried about what might be in the water.

"Bring me a Dr. Pepper if you have one, if not a Coke will do." It looked like he would be sticking with soda for now.

"Going for the hard stuff I see." Sarcasm dripped onto the table. "I'll be back with your drinks and get your food orders unless you're filling up on the condiments." Whoa, what a sassy waitress. She probably wasn't used to being tipped well in this place so made no effort. Pax noted that the woman's personality fit the gritty environment as she swished her hips around on exit. He turned his attention back to the woman he was actually attracted to seated at his table, the one wearing much less revealing clothing.

"Where do we go from here? Should I start canvassing the room?"

"Let's just act natural and see where it takes us." Luna suggested.

Their server eventually returned depositing their drinks between them, then pulled out her order pad and pen without a word. Pax noticed a name tag that he had somehow missed earlier displayed on her hip instead of her bare chest since there wasn't enough fabric to pin it there.

"Thank you, Trixie. I'll have the Star Burger with fries." Pax spoke slowly pretty sure that Trixie was not the waitress's real name, perhaps a professional one suggesting that she turned tricks too?

Trixie turned her head to look at Luna and nodded. "I guess I'll try the Surprise Sandwich with a fruit cup." Luna was probably hoping that the surprise was healthier than the identifiable options listed on the menu. Trixie's chuckle led Pax to believe Luna's assumption was wrong. He soon turned out to be correct.

Pax's plate arrived with the burger he expected. However, Luna's dish displayed an open-faced sandwich on pumpernickel rye bread with sardines stretched across it staring up at her from a blanket of lettuce. He must admit the fish did look surprised. The fruit cup smelled of liquor as if soaking in it helped the fish heads slide down the customer's gullet easier. Pax was curious to see what Luna would say about the food set before her when his unflappable friend side-stepped the whole odd entre topic and coolly let the unusual meal be an ice breaker leading into their intended endeavor.

"Trixie, we were sorry to hear about the untimely death of your mayor." Was Luna guessing that the mayor had probably eaten here at times due to proximity and that in some way had contributed to his demise? But their server's response was one they had not anticipated.

"Yeah, well, most people 'round here were just surprised it didn't happen sooner." And bingo, they were in.

The rest of the afternoon proceeded similarly. They would sincerely apologize to the locals for the death of their mayor and no one seemed to be shocked or especially sad that it had happened. It appeared Mayor Dankworth was not the shining political figure he appeared to be to the outside world. It sounded like even his ex-wives were believed to possess plenty of motive for wanting the guy gone. There was definitely more to this story. The amateur detectives dropped into two more eating establishments to continue their progressive diner search.

At the first, the sleuths just ordered tea so Luna could compare the warm liquid with her blends. The diner's cups bearing teabags were so terrible that she decided to give the shift manager her card with a ten percent discount on his first order of Ferns-Bee Teas telling him that he would not be sorry if he gave them a try. However, besides the perk of a possible new customer, they found no new info about the mayor, just more apathy at his death, so the two moved on.

Late afternoon Pax and Luna walked into Polly's Pies hoping to end their Starville date with a dessert fix for Pax's sweet tooth. Polly served all sorts of pies. Her breakfast pies looked more like cheese quiche, while the lunch and dinner menu options offered a long list of various meat and vegetable-filled pastries. An additional twenty flavors of fruit and cream-filled pies were listed for dessert.

Pax picked out a chocolate-peanut butter cream pie and wished he gotten two slices after the first bite. Luna was enjoying a lighter lemon-coconut combination of flavors when an unfamiliar man stopped by their table.

"I heard you mention the mayor to your waitress." His comment sounded more like a question.

"Yes, we wanted to express our sorrow for Starville's loss." Luna stuck with their scripted comment.

"That's not necessary believe me. I noticed that you've been hanging around the area and assume you're looking for information. Be careful. Start with the accountant's books and not the ones he gives the IRS. You'll find more of what or who you are looking for off-the-books or in those cooked under the counter if you know what I mean." The man tipped his hat and slipped out the restaurant's door.

"That was strange." Pax admitted. "You don't think it was a trap, do you?"

"No, I think that the mayor is not as well-liked as the outside world has been led to believe. From our little visit today, we've learned there are many who supposedly didn't mind at all that the man died, some of whom might be suspects. This latest tip sounds like the killer could be intertwined in his business dealings. We need to stop by and see Aiden. Let's go." Luna started to stand up.

"I have time to finish my pie, Birdwhistle isn't going anywhere." Ending their date by sharing Luna with his competition was not Pax's first choice, but he'd had nearly the whole day alone with her. Paying a call at the jailhouse would allow more time with Luna and at least they'd be on the same side of the bars. Pax savored the ride there with his counterfeit date as much as the lingering taste of his pie. Aiden Birdwhistle was casually eating cake when they arrived.

"I can share," he offered.

"We just had dessert," Luna quickly responded, or Pax would have been open for round two.

"Looks like they feed you quite fancy here for county incarceration." Pax noted not feeling so bad for the guy.

"This cake wasn't provided by the county I assure you. I seem to have acquired my own personal baker and am not complaining." Aiden admitted.

"We just dropped by for a quick visit to inform you about a few things that we found on our first espionage attempts." It sounded like Luna was also planning on a round two but with the detective work, not dessert.

"I'm impressed. Thanks, guys." Aiden set down his cake focusing his full attention on the two of them.

"Don't be Birdwhistle. They're pretty vague." Pax didn't want to get the guy's hopes up.

"Well, we found out the mayor was not popular. Many people didn't like him and may have had less than positive intentions or possibly harmful motives towards him. Tell your lawyer to check out his ex-wives and his accountant's books looking for business partners." Luna shared.

"The books kept off the record. Not the ones the prosecution has probably seen." Pax added.

"I'll see what I can do with those tips. My lawyer is not exactly what you would call the cream of the crop or at the top of his field, but anything is helpful at this point. I'll pass it along." Having finished his cake, Aiden's cell looked somehow bleaker.

"We won't give up on you." Luna shared. Even Pax wished they had more to offer the poor guy. He looked pretty forlorn.

The sky was rapidly draining of light as they drove and arrived back at the treehouse. Sherlock began his happy dance even before Luna emerged from the car. Not wanting the dog to soak up all of the affection after such a great day together, Pax stepped out of his SUV with the words, "Let me walk you to your door and finish this fake date right."

Luna laughed her enchantingly lyrical laugh, "You really are into this uncover persona."

Pax followed her up the ramp that he had built to the top and stood straddling the narrow strip of a makeshift plank porch. Their bodies pressed awkwardly close together as she pulled out her key. "I'm not sure I want this day to end," he admitted.

"We can go again next weekend if you'd like. We got some great leads. I think we're getting close and Aiden seemed so hopeful." Pax didn't want the evening to end focused on Bridwhistle even if most of the day had been. He could see the outline of Luna's perfect profile with a slightly upturned nose silhouetted against the dimming sky. Still in the throes of their magical day, Pax spoke boldly.

"How about ending our spy mission with a little fake kiss to finish off the fake date?"

Luna didn't say yes, or even speak at all, but gently tilted her head upwards towards his. The feeling of connection must be contagious. Both of their past hesitancy seemed to evaporate into the night air. Pax felt Luna's cheek brush his before their lips found each other. The soft sweetness of her mouth melted into his. Emotions aroused immediately, dang he was going to have to stop before he wasn't able to, and Luna's response was one hundred percent in. If she was just playing out the closing scene from her role today, she was very convincing. Her body relaxed into his and Pax had to hold her up, it was as if Luna had become a little weak in the knees. Finally, a glimpse of hope beyond platonic.

"Goodnight my Watson," Pax whispered into Luna's ear knowing that she would get the reference, even though he was more the Watson of their team. It was better to leave a woman wanting more than with regret for anything that might happen he convinced himself. "Let me know what our next move is." She could wonder as she sipped her tea tonight if the 'next move' he referenced had to do with the save-Aiden mission or the fake date becoming more real. Their chest board was getting more complicated.

He felt her lips still pressed against his face draw into a smile as she replied huskily, "Yes, I'll definitely do that."

Surpassing Herculean effort, Pax forced himself to gently release Luna steadying her on both feet before exiting down the ramp. It was going to be a long ride home alone tonight.

Chapter 12

__There are spacecrafts observing the Sun right now.__ The most famous spacecraft sent to observe the Sun is the Solar and Heliospheric Observatory, built by NASA and ESA, and launched in December 1995. SOHO has been continuously observing the Sun since then and has sent back countless images. A more recent mission is NASA's STEREO spacecraft. This mission launched two spacecrafts in October 2006. These twin spacecrafts were designed to watch the same activity on the Sun from two different vantage points to give a 3-D perspective of the Sun's activity and allow astronomers to better predict space weather.

Aiden

Aiden felt like he had become one of those organ grinder's monkeys where their owners dress them up in little suits and lead around on a rope to perform at their beck and call. Last week had been his arraignment, followed by a pretrial conference and now today was his preliminary hearing. His parents brought him a nice suit and tie to replace his jailhouse garb whenever he was paraded out in front of the court to portray the clean-cut appearance of an upstanding young man…which was what he actually was whether dressed in the outfit or not. Then the family would sit solemnly on a courtroom bench. His mother with a hanky dabbing her eyes. His dad with the 'go-get-em-son' look he always wore watching from the stands whenever Aiden competed, the only thing missing was the occasional fist-pump. And his little brother looking mostly bored with this whole legal part of the process. Uncle Toby had become his official organ grinder who held the end of the imaginary chain around Aiden's neck.

The arraignment had gone okay he guessed. Up until the very last minute his not-so-esteemed lawyer, Mr. Berrycloth, had persisted in trying to convince Aiden that he needed to make some kind of plea bargain. Aiden knew he was innocent and refused to budge on that issue. He had to maintain his core principles even as a prisoner. No jury was present at the arraignment. The courtroom contained one judge, the prosecutor, his defense counsel with defendant…him…along with a few other potential defendants and their counsels waiting for their turns to face the court. A small contingency from the general public was also present. His last court appearance had been a ghost town compared to this current event. It appeared that voyeurs had crawled out of the woodwork to watch what happened in his preliminary hearing.

Aiden's previous not-guilty plea had not gone over well. Uncle Toby would have preferred that Aiden enter a no-contest plea at the very least, which was still basically a guilty plea so Aiden couldn't do it. The only difference in a no-contest plea was that he, the accused, would be stating that he was not going to fight the charges against himself but was not admitting to any guilt. It had the same legal ramifications as a guilty plea and Aiden wouldn't go there.

Toby insisted that the benefit of a no-contest plea… where you admit the facts, but not your guilt…is that it allows you to avoid a trial if your defense has become hopeless and prevents the plea from being used against you in any later civil or criminal proceeding. Aiden thought his family affiliated lawyer was just plain lazy and that his uncle didn't want to have to work to prove his innocence. But Aiden was innocent. His own lawyer should at least believe in him and spare him the legalese BS.

At his arraignment, the judge had read aloud the formal criminal charges against Aiden Birdwhitle, then asked how he wanted to plead.

Aiden responded with a bold, "NOT GUILTY your Honor."

However, the case could not be dismissed on grounds of a shaky foundation as his lawyer had not even bothered to file a motion to have the case dropped. Nor was a release granted or any bail set. A future court date had been established for a preliminary hearing since his crime was considered a felony case. That set date was today.

Following his depressing formal arraignment, where Aiden had felt like the ultimate underdog, he and his inadequate criminal defense attorney had appeared for a brief pretrial conference. There the judge had informed them that if the defendant was found guilty, a sentence would be handed down and that the death penalty was not off the table. Life in prison was the best outcome they could probably hope for if convicted. The good news just kept rolling in. With luck, Luna or someone else would uncover new evidence soon, if not Aiden would have to drown his sorrows in cake.

His parents and Rocco sat stoically on their same pew-like bench. They were his own small cheering section for the continuing courtroom drama. It was nice to have their support. Maybe the experience would inspire Rocco to be an attorney. He would probably be better than their uncle right now without any schooling. Perhaps Aiden was being a little tough on Tobias Berrycloth but it certainly didn't seem like it.

His rumpled attorney arrived with a short stack of paperwork and began to sort through it. "Let's see, it says that the preliminary hearing is like a mini-trial. Hmmm...a preliminary hearing is best described as a 'trial before the trial' at which the judge decides, not whether the defendant is guilty or not guilty, but whether there is enough evidence to force the defendant to stand trial. In contrast, the arraignment is where the defendant may file their pleas. Yep, we've already done that."

The man was actually reading right now what he was supposed to do at this hearing. Heaven help them, sheesh, did his uncle even know where they were, why they were there or what they were doing? What was the plan to get him off?? Aiden began to wonder if representing himself would be better than this buffoon.

Uncle Toby continued reading, "The prosecution will call witnesses and introduce evidence, and the defense can cross-examine witnesses. If the judge concludes there is probable cause to believe the crime was committed by the defendant, a trial will soon be scheduled... Okay, that sounds good, we've got this. I'm glad we don't have to have our own witnesses yet."

"Toby, did you even look into any of the information that I mentioned Luna shared with me? She could be a witness for us. And there should only be circumstantial evidence on me since I didn't do it. Remember? This shouldn't be that hard."

"Of course, I just wish we had that murder weapon." Aiden dropped his head into his hands wondering if his lawyer uncle ever heard a word he said. He looked back at his family and gave them a weak smile. Did they realize that they had sentenced their son to certain doom?

The prosecution, not surprisedly, was more prepared than the defense team. The mayor's secretary was first called to the witness stand stating that Aiden Birdwhistle had been the only appointment that the mayor had scheduled before that time of the morning…that time? … the time of his death when she had found his body… the woman stumbled along with her words and then broke into tears and could not continue.

Another witness shared that Aiden's work truck had been spotted parked near the scene of the crime that morning. Of course, it had, he did not deny being there and who could miss the bright yellow vehicle with unique signage across its side. There, that should be more proof, if he had wanted to kill the guy and get away with it would he have driven there in his personal calling card.

The police detective's testimony was the most damaging. Officer Oswald shared with the court that they had not found any other suspects at this time, not only was no one else scheduled or seen in the office or its vicinity but Aiden's prints were discovered in the room and on the body. Again, Aiden noted, would the killer have made an appointment? And his fingerprints were there because he had tried to see if he could save the man. So much for being a good Samaritan.

The officer continued that there were signs of a brief scuffle...*but not with him Aiden wanted to scream*...and the fatal wound was created with force, so forensics believe it was most likely done by a strong male...*or anyone with large amounts adrenaline coursing through their veins Aiden mentally added.* The autopsy showed no signs of heart failure or any unusual drugs in his system that may have contributed to his death. The murder appeared to have happened shortly after Mayor Dankworth ate his breakfast as crumbs were found on his desk and the cleaners had been there the night before, so the remnants of food were new.

Aiden nudged his uncle, "Aren't you going to cross exam the detective?"

"Well, what he shared is pretty much all fact, how do you disagree with facts?"

"How about, Aiden himself has admitted to all of those things, but that does not omit the fact that another person could also have been in the room before him and committed the crime!" Aiden spoke loud enough for the whole room to hear him. From his outburst, the judge was compelled to ask if either Mr. Birdwhistle or his lawyer had any questions that they would like to ask the witness.

"If you don't, I will." Aiden lowered his voice so only his attorney could hear him this time.

Without enthusiasm Tobias Berrycloth rose to address the witness asking Aiden's suggestions and even throwing in a few half-hearted inquiries of his own. But not enough to sway the emotions of the room. In the end, the verdict was that Aiden Birdwhistle was going to be prosecuted for the crime of murder in the first degree. The prosecution had slaughtered them in round one.

Aiden turned around to look back at his family all lined up in a row. His mother was no longer dabbing at her tears but trying to dam up the flood that drained down her face with her handkerchief. His dad was insensitively blaming his mother for her brother's incompetence and Aiden's own brother looked the most animated that he had since the preliminary hearing began. Rocco was probably envisioning his brother's capital crime splashed across the front pages of newspapers and clogging up social media, too immature to realize that fame or infamy was not always a positive thing and didn't always end happily ever after.

Pushing past the barrier through the gate that separated the criminals and those who debated their fates from those here to observe, Aiden didn't wait to ask permission. The apathetic bailiff could try to stop him with his nerf gun or billy club if he wanted to. Aiden was going to attempt to comfort his deeply distressed mother whose sobs had turned into loud hiccups.

"Does this mean you won't be home for Thanksgiving?" Mrs. Birdwhistle gasped out between sobs. Thanksgiving was the least of his worries, Aiden didn't have the heart to tell her there was a chance he would never be coming home again, forget about missing Thanksgiving.

"Doesn't look like it right now, mom, but you can bring me a plate of all my favorite leftovers. Leftovers are the best anyway." He embraced her convulsing body circling it with his arms. Aiden knew his mother understood the reality of what he was facing, she was a bright woman, but neither of them wanted to express the possibilities out loud. That would make the situation all too real.

His father patted him on the shoulder with a non-convincing, "things will be okay, son."

His brother still appeared far too happy about the whole situation. Teenage emotions were a mystery. Maybe it was the excitement of the adventure along with the underlying belief that they were immortal and nothing bad could ever happen to them or to those they loved.

The bailiff joined their dreary family circle to let Aiden know it was time to take him back to the jail. Could the guy give them a moment? The man didn't look like he would starve if he was late for dinner or missed a meal now and then. Aiden looked for his uncle to ask him to intervene and give the fam a few more minutes together, but Uncle Toby had already disappeared. Hopefully to go work on their case since he had given such a poor performance in the courtroom today. More likely because he was embarrassed by said performance and didn't want to face his sister.

"Alright, alright, I'm almost ready." Then Aiden let himself be led away realizing that his destiny was no longer in his own hands and he didn't have more to say to his family anyway.

The court officer who could use some time on a treadmill or Stairmaster if his snail crawl pace was any indication, escorted Aiden Birdwhistle back to his sparsely decorated cell and into his jailhouse jumpsuit. Aiden would no longer be a temporary resident in Moonburg's jail. It was now official; he would remain here at the county seat while awaiting his final outcome. Redecorating was in order. It was time to build a more comfy nest in his now long-term habitat. Environment makes a difference.

CITY TWO

Moonburg

Existence is a balancing act in the ultimate middle ground on a moor subsisting between the highlands and the lowlands. Surrounding my habitat grow temperate grasslands, savannas, and shrublands covering the hills with low-growing vegetation in acidic soil. Moorlands are basically uncultivated hills but can include low-lying wetlands. I sprung up between both. Heaths are considered cousins of mine, but I'm not sure how we are related. We are similar; however, my land gets more rainfall and humans often have to lend heaths a helping hand.

The moor may be the natural environment where I live, but much of my construction or existence is man-made. I am considered the county seat or the central hub of this geographical region and cover more square miles than any other city in the area. Nearly all would deem me the most diverse due to the college and private prep school that are housed here. Moonbeam University (MU) and an internationally renowned private prep-school named Beam Academy found permanent homes within my midst. Major technology businesses were born from academic proximity allowing easy acquisition of educated employees who would not need to relocate. I take pride in being a place of vast learning and cradling learned people in my valleys. The students add to my depth.

Unfortunately, some of the scholars who inhabit me believe that they know everything when I can guarantee that they still have much to learn. I could give them an extra lesson or two if they were willing to tune in and listen to what surrounds them. Knowledge is a good thing if used for good. Some residents here are quite wise, others use their learning to look down on those who don't have as much. These happenings are hard to observe from my limited position to intercede. I guess I could quake and cause collapses, but two wrongs don't make a right and it would be painful for myself as well. Still, I want to shake or wake things up at times. Competition is common, but I find it disappointing that most want to be better than the next person not merely better to improve themselves.

Even their adornments are often superficial. Give me a simple bucket of paint any day. Clothes on Moonburgers are not focused on function but more for show. It is like putting peacock feathers on a pig. Even though common sense is at a premium, they are still mine, so I nurture them with all I have to offer and enjoy being part of their accomplishments. Luna Fernsby is one of the good ones, but she now lives on my outskirts barely within my sprawling boundaries. I still count her as my own and wish there were more like her. Pax Loughty resides in that same category of humans and he works to keep Luna connected to the vital parts of me. The people who reside within any area create its true spirit and pulse.

Shiny is the best description of the dwellings where these flesh and blood moonbeams live and work and shop. Not many structures are of mortar and brick, most buildings are wood sided with false facades. Stucco is also becoming popular. I am considered attractive by most who live here or even those passing through. It does not make me vain. To be clean and neat and tidy is my preference. Beauty is just an added benefit and I don't let it go to my rooftops.

Lately I have been feeling growth pains hopefully without the dreaded stretch marks. Technology has been booming everywhere and I.T. businesses have flooded my area to take advantage of the location and lifestyle here. Our airport just added another wing to manage the increased number of flights in and out by students and remote workers who occasionally must visit their places of employment and not just connect via the computer screen. Vacationers heading up to my sister Sunlight City also fly into my location since I possess a more level runway for landings and can handle the larger international planes. There is a rumor that a second college may spring up among us soon as well. Yes, I am the most prolific of the three solar loop sisters. Middle children are usually the easiest to reside around.

If I could change anything it would be to allow more diversity on the moor. Not diversity of race, we do well in that sector. Immigrants from all over the world come to take advantage of the educational opportunities we have to offer. No, I am speaking of more diversity of thought. Ironically, those that believe themselves to be the most liberal in their thinking are often the least accepting of those who do not follow their same thought patterns and processes. We need to be better at celebrating and embracing uniqueness in whatever arena.

Chapter 13

The average distance from the Moon to the Earth is 384,403 kilometers or 238,857 miles. Unlike the Earth, the Moon has no atmosphere. This means that the Moon is unprotected from cosmic rays, meteorites, solar winds, and has huge temperature variations. The lack of atmosphere means no sound can be heard on the Moon, and the sky always appears black. The Moon is very hot during the day but very cold at night. The average surface temperature of the Moon is 107 degrees Celsius during the day and -153 degrees Celsius at night.

Zori

The jail cell had blossomed a bit taking upon a homier appearance. A quilt with square patches cut from Aiden's old t-shirts exhibiting his favorite bands and high school sports teams had been sewn together by his mother and now covered the cot. Topped by a pillowcase-less pillow to prevent him from hiding foreign objects inside of it. Books, cards, and a box of teabags sat on the stool beside his bed. Zori didn't take Aiden for a tea-man but was glad if the warm liquid gave him comfort and something to wash down her desserts. She had been coming biweekly to Moonburg for the past few months and sometimes three times a week. Not only making tandem trips when coming to her classes at the college but also whenever she had a long enough window of time off work to enable her to drop by. The portion sizes of the treats she brought... lemon tarts, snickerdoodles, German chocolate cupcakes... had become smaller as not to encourage waste, diabetes, or obesity. She had lost count of all the things she had delivered to Aiden, so started keeping a list to keep her from doubling up on the delicacies unless requested.

Today she had merely picked up chocolate milkshakes for both of them when she got into town. Zori loved to serve ice cream on her baked goods, but ice cream did not travel well, so she was mixing it up with the new option. She hoped their conversations were as much food for his psyche as her baked wares were for his stomach. Her desire was to feed or refresh his whole soul with her visits. The amazing part was that she felt as if she was getting far more from the experience than she was giving. Their time together gave Zori unique glimpses of herself and she liked the way she looked through Aiden's eyes. She even liked Aiden...in fact she liked him a lot. Zori shared more about herself with him than she ever had with anyone else, and she felt so atypically comfortable around the guy.

The guards must not think that Aiden was much of a threat or flight risk. They allowed Zori to play cards with him through the bars of his cell to pass the time as they visited. Keeping her hands and brain busy on something besides their discussion distracted her from the fact her mouth was opening and spewing out things she might not have been totally okay telling him had she been fulling concentrating on their conversation.

Today they were playing a rousing game of King's Corner. It was challenging to fit the deck of cards onto the stool with the descending rows of numerical values alternating between red and black. They had squished up the piles with the cards stacked on top of each other so only the card facing upward on top was visible to prevent the whole stack from falling onto the cement floor. It worked. King's Corner wasn't a difficult game, mindless enough that they could talk about most anything and not miss a play too often. Gin Rummy, War and Go Fish were also good go-to games. For Hearts, they really needed more players. Zori and Aiden were equally matched in their card skill levels so took turns winning. No bets were ever placed. The games were all for fun.

Zori played the last card she held in her hand. A black ace of spades laid gently on top of a red two of hearts so that the pile didn't slide off the stool. She had won the game. Looking up with a smile Zori asked her opponent, "Would you like to try poker next? We haven't played that yet. Maybe a round of five-card stud? Or we can wait until next time and I'll bring M&Ms to bet with." The thought came into her mind that they could play strip poker and discard items of clothing for their bets if they lost a hand. A deep red flush spread across her face even though she had not spoken the words aloud. Thank goodness! What was wrong with her smutty brain. The card game would be questionable enough in the privacy of one of their homes but here in a public building, it would be quite scandalous. Their discovery would make quite a tantalizing headline…*Murder Suspect with Card Playing Opponent Caught Naked with Bars Between*. Yikes.

"We can wait for you to bring the reward system to bet with, but I feel bad that you contribute so much each time you come. Just your visits are really enough… quite wonderful actually." Aiden's words sounded sincere. "I'm not even sure to what grand fate of the universe I owe your guardian angel-ship. What inspired you to start coming in the first place?"

How could Zori answer that question when she wasn't exactly sure of the real reason herself. She gracefully side-stepped answering with a quick quip and then asked a question of her own, "Blame the newscasters for my incessant visits. The handsome photo they dug up to splash across the television screen made me want to see if you were for real and the rest is history. I kept coming because you are actually pretty pathetic." Zori chortled to let him know she was kidding, "But really, what do you do all day in here and what do you think about with all the free time you have alone? I'm sure it's hard." She wasn't really expecting a serious response.

"Honestly, it sucks a lot of the time. But I've gotten to know myself better without all of the distractions that I used to fill my days with. The biggest challenge is not feeling too sorry for myself. You've helped a ton with that. On some of my darkest days, you've walked down the hallway and made all the difference. Truly."

Zori felt tears in her eyes that she would not let fall. He was such a good guy and so grateful for her simple efforts. "Do you think you'll be different when you get out of here?"

"Don't you mean *if* I get out of here? I sure hope so. If I haven't learned anything I deserve to stay inside until I do. I wasted so much time before. Now I have time to waste but I don't want to."

"Maybe you could take college classes while you are in here? Students can get degrees online these days. I bet you could get permission to have a laptop computer. It would probably need to have a zillion filters on it but that'd be okay. You wouldn't be wasting time but using it to become better. What would you want to study? I could bring a catalog of the degrees offered at MU."

"If I never get out, what's the point?" Aiden sounded slightly hopeful despite his question.

"Haven't you ever heard that the mind is an awful thing to waste? You'll take that brain with you wherever you go, and you can't give up on your future yet." Zori suddenly felt intense about this. She almost wanted Aiden to get a degree more than she wanted one for herself. "So, what sounds interesting to study?"

"Well, I used to want to become a coach and teach history or P.E. since my coaches made such a difference in my life, but if things don't change the only place that I would be able to use that degree is developing an exercise program for calisthenics in the prison yard." Aiden glumly noted.

"That could still be beneficial, but is there anything else that comes to mind?" She pressed.

"You know, there is, I actually have a desire to study law. My uncle could certainly use the help."

"Isn't he doing a good job on your case?" Zori was curious.

"Unfortunately, the man is awful. I considered asking for a court-appointed attorney to replace him, but that would create an excrement hailstorm in the family, and Uncle Toby has to get some points for caring about me. A stranger would be representing me merely for the fee."

"I wonder if I could talk my dad into sponsoring your representation. He has a lot of money and could afford a high-caliber attorney." Zori was amused by Aiden's avoidance of swearing in her presence and she wasn't at all sure her father would be willing to do anything of the kind. Marcus MacQuiod may consider it a conflict of interest to protect someone else from a crime that he might need defending from himself, but she really wanted to help somehow.

"I wouldn't feel okay asking that from a man I don't even know, but it is extremely generous of you to offer."

"If you change your mind let me know. For now, you can start with pre-law classes and then apply to a law school at some point. Does that sound like a plan?" Zori had morphed into guidance counselor mode. Aiden had nothing but time. In twenty years, he could still be sitting in here as a convict, or he could have become a convicted lawyer who sets himself free. Yes, this was the most productive path either of them had started on in months. "So, you start working on getting permission for a laptop approved and, in the meantime, I'll bring you a course catalog and registration forms to get you going."

"Again, I'm not sure what to say besides thanks. It's awkward to have one's whole life in the hands of others, mercy at the hands of strangers you know. Please know I'm extremely grateful."

Their card games were over for now, but Zori wasn't quite ready to leave. Here inside the protected walls of the jail, she felt like she had more to offer the world than outside in her real life.

"Does anyone else visit you?" Zori wondered if she was Aiden's sole fan club member.

"My family comes about once a week. My dad has to work extra hours now with me in here. Although some of our business has dropped off due to my current circumstances. Not everyone is okay with a murder suspect or even his father hanging around their home. It makes my mom too sad to see me like this on a daily basis and I'm mostly a sideshow for my younger brother. If they lived in town, I'm sure they'd be here more often. Then there's my attorney uncle and a few new friends I've made that stop by. Luna and Pax live in or near Moonburg so are closer. I spent a day on the lamb at Luna's treehouse. Long story, but she tended to my injuries and gave me time to gather my thoughts while I was a fugitive from the law. You guys are my only regulars."

Zori noticed a surge of jealousy rise in her chest even though the female's name was paired with a man's and choked out her concern. "Are you pretty close to Luna and Pax?"

"They're really the only ones who believe I'm innocent, that I know of, besides you. I just assumed you don't think I did it. Doubt you'd be here if you did. They're looking for other leads in my case. I know it's a long shot but they're willing to help me and even have a dog named Sherlock." Aiden sounded as if he was reaching for straws at this point.

"I do believe in you Mr. Aiden Birdwhistle and am sure others do too. We're going to get you registered at the university and on the road to becoming an attorney at law. So even if Uncle Toby lets you down, you will be able to resurrect yourself one day." It sounded like the friend duo was off fighting crime on the outside. Zori would be an advocate for the accused right here on the inside, at his side.

She had been hanging out at the jail for nearly two hours already. Bribed by baked goods the guards had gotten lenient on the length of her visits. A Betty Crocker wannabe did not seem a likely candidate to mastermind a jail breakout. Zori was not so sure; she might be capable of planning an escape if it looked like Aiden would be condemned to a life behind bars or worse. She had surprised herself a lot lately.

Guess I gotta go. My shift at the dealership starts in an hour, I'll have to drive straight there as it is, but I'll be back soon."

"Thanks. I know you will, and I'll look forward to it." Aiden responded gratefully.

At times it felt harder for her to leave than it would be for him, and Aiden was locked in. Dragging herself away Zori drove home pondering the recent chain of events in her life. She had begun visiting the jail on a whim, out of curiosity, and then continued going due to compassion as she got to know Aiden better. The original plan had been to bring him treats and catch a quick peek, not to speak with him. She wasn't sure why she was compelled to go in the first place. It was foolish. But now she really liked Aiden, maybe too much. Zori was afraid she was falling for him or had already tumbled off of that cliff. She had never felt this way about any guy before. Not that she was an expert in the area of romantic relationships. She had dated and even kissed other guys. A few of those extended kisses could probably be considered full-on make-out sessions and she had even gotten to second base with one boy but had never liked any enough to let them score a home run off her.

Having a mom to talk to about boy things would make life easier. Or perhaps even better a girlfriend who was emotionally close enough and more experienced in love life matters than herself to ask the private inquiries that she grappled with. Any female figure would be helpful. In reality, girls probably didn't ask their mothers much about boys anyway and definitely not their dads unless they wanted those same fathers to carry around a shotgun for chasing off the handsy ones. That would definitely not be good, her dad didn't need another murder on his hands or his conscience.

Chapter 14

The Moon is a fifth-largest natural satellite in our solar system. At 3,475 km in diameter, the Moon is much smaller than the major moons of Jupiter and Saturn. A prevailing theory is that the Moon was once part of the Earth and was formed from a chunk that broke away due to a huge object colliding with Earth when it was relatively young.

Aiden

There was something curious about the girl from Starville. Not just her faded-out coloring that looked as if she were washed a few more times in cycles of laundry she would come out an albino. Or the fact that she brought a perfect stranger baked goods several times a week when she didn't even live in Moonburg. She was not a friend or former girlfriend from his hometown either for that matter. No, it was more the things that she didn't talk about and the fact she was willing to talk about nothing at all for long periods of time and just watch him with her pale blue eyes. He was not sure Zori could be described as stunning, but she was definitely striking as well as ultra-kind and a master listener. She may not have been the type of girl he would have dated before jail time, but Aiden could see them spending time together when he got out…if he got out. If he never got out, he wondered if would she continue to bring him goodies and visit with him for the next twenty-plus years? For some reason, the idea would not surprise him. She seemed extraordinarily committed.

Zori had recently dropped by a few decorations that met the approved inmate guidelines for the holidays in an attempt to make his cell feel more festive. Of course, the décor was accompanied by a baked treat of peppermint frosted Christmas cookies. Yes, the girl was a shining jewel in his cave of wonders. Zori had insisted that she would be visiting him on Christmas Day explaining that her family didn't do much for any of the holidays so she would rather bring him some Christmas cheer than sit at home. So, he would see her again tomorrow.

It was Christmas Eve; Aiden would be celebrating the yuletide evening in jail tonight. His ornament-less miniature Christmas tree with attached white lights emitted a soft glow from its height-enhancing spot on the stool. His family had come to share their annual Christmas Eve festivities, which though the event looked much different this year, would carry on the family tradition. It was the Birdwhistle's designated time to gather, usually after a delicious hot meal around the table leaving Christmas Day reserved for total relaxation in their home. Relaxation shouldn't be a problem for him here on his cot. The family brought Aiden a plate of dinner that had gotten cold on the drive but still tasted great and caused many memories of Christmases past to erupt via his taste buds.

His father opened the family Bible and read chapter two out of the book of Luke containing the story of Christ's birth. The blessed expectant couple had already gone to Bethlehem to be taxed and Mary had given birth in a stable since there was no room for them at the inn. The angels were now announcing the baby savior's birth to the shepherds. His dad's deep voice resonated off of the cement walls... *"the glory of the Lord shone round about them: and they were sore afraid. And the angel said unto them, Fear not: for, behold, I bring you tidings of great joy, which shall be to all people. For unto you is born this day in the city of David a Savior, which is Christ the Lord. And this shall be a sign unto you; Ye shall find the babe wrapped in swaddling clothes, lying in a manger. And suddenly there was with the angel a multitude of the heavenly host praising God, and saying, Glory to God in the highest, and on earth peace, goodwill toward men."*

Where was an angel telling Aiden not to be afraid when he needed one? If Jesus was born in a stable, Aiden's warm, dry cell suddenly didn't seem so bad. Maybe his angels were around, just not as glorious or as heavenly as the ones in the Bible, perhaps they came to him in earthly disguise. He needed to not feel so sorry for himself and recognize the people who did bless his life. Aiden looked around at his family who were attempting to bring him holiday cheer and a lump welled up in his throat. They were salt of the earth people and probably suffering nearly as much as he was right now. They may not be literally behind these bars, but society had placed them in prisons of their own due to his arrest. Besides Rocco, who still seemed to be utterly enjoying his brief ride aboard the infamy train.

The Birdwhistles pressed on with their regularly scheduled activities attempting a feeble caroling session. None of them were solo singers but together the sound wasn't so bad. Aiden's favorite Christmas carol had always been *Silent Night*, so his mom had planned to end the set of songs with it. However, the classic song sounded extremely melancholy tonight with the iron bars hovering between them. His mother suggested they sing one more and end their Christmas chorus with a more upbeat melody. The family vocally dashed through non-existent snow, maybe not laughing all the way like in *Jingle Bells* but the bouncy melody at least putting smiles on their faces in spite of the dreary surroundings.

The party had proceeded less than an hour when Aiden could feel his family getting restless. There was not much in the way of creature comforts to offer them in this environment. Nothing about the surroundings screamed Merry Christmas. The guards had tried to find an alternate room where the family could meet minus the incarcerated feeling of the cell, but the jail staff was low in numbers tonight due to the holiday and there were not any extra personnel available to monitor a separate gathering.

"Well, son we wanted to wish you a Merry Christmas," Never one for long goodbyes his father extended his calloused hand through the bars and shook his son's softening one. Not much manual labor was required in here.

His little brother handed him a wrapped gift which felt like a book hiding inside the Santa splattered paper. Aiden definitely had time for reading in here. Curious what Rocco thought would be a good distraction for him, Aiden ripped off the wrapping paper to uncover a Sherlock Holmes mystery. Not exactly what he was hoping for, but nonetheless Aiden thanked them for the present. Unless they gave him a file or softer toilet paper, an item more useful was hard to find.

"Yeah, I thought a murder mystery might be right up your alley these days and who knows, it may give you some ideas on solving your case." Rocco expressed triumphantly like he had hit the jackpot of practical gifts when a mind-numbing romance would have been more appreciated. A love story might be able to take Aiden's mind away from the darkness that was clogging it at all hours.

With tears in her eyes his mother reached in and pulled his face towards hers planting gentle kisses on his forehead. "Things will be okay, my dear Aiden. I know they will. I'm not sure how that will happen, but I pray for you every day."

More for her, than himself, Aiden answered, "I'm sure they will, mom. Don't worry." When actually Aiden was not sure at all. That would have to be his Christmas gift to her for now. Belief. It was the best he could give and came from the heart. The trio didn't give him an official goodbye but slowly wandered down the hall away from the dismal scene of their caged loved one. Even the Christmas decorations hadn't muted the harshness of the situation.

It was still too early to try to sleep. Aiden would end up staring at the ceiling for who knows how long. He opened the book they had left for him and started to page through it reading by the light of tiny tree bulbs. There was one full-length novel and several short story mysteries contained between the front and back covers. Sir Arthur Conan Doyle would get him through the night. The story eerily shadowed his reality. A male corpse is discovered and identified to be a very wealthy man; however, this corpse was named Enoch Drebber, not Mayor Dankworth. Blood is found in the room with the victim, ditto, but there is no wound on the body in the book, making its discovery more mysterious than the blood from the mayor's obviously bludgeoned corpse. Holmes also learns from documents found on the book-body that the deceased was traveling in London with his secretary. Written on one wall in red near the body, was "RACHE". Aiden wished the actual killer in Starville had left a message to help unravel the real-life whodunit that he had unwittingly become a character in. After reading about as much of the mystery he could take in one sitting, footsteps could be heard coming down the corridor. Conceivably, it was a guard taking some kind of mercy on him in honor of the holiday. Instead of a guard's unfriendly mug, Luna and Pax appeared large as life outside of his cell.

"To what do I owe this Christmas mini-miracle?" Aiden grinned getting up off the cot to greet them.

"I'm sure you're well aware of Luna's charms, not many can say no to this girl it seems." Like that explained their presence but Pax continued, "She may yet get us both arrested for breaking into a secure area at the newspaper to use some super-servers that are usually beyond access to those of my peon employee status. So, there's a chance we could be joining you in here in the near future," Pax grimaced. Aiden was still not fully following Pax's storyline as the big guy took a breath and continued, "And just now she convinced the officers to allow us a quick visit since it was Christmas Eve and all. She couldn't enjoy our Christmas until we stopped by to say hi." Pax, quite unusual for himself, had opened the other side of the conversation leaving Aiden not clearly comprehending most of anything he was trying to tell him.

"We may not be official wisemen, but with Pax's connections at the newspaper and maybe a little extra ingenuity on my part, we made some headway into the 'other possible suspects' category. Names for your legal team to investigate further... as your Christmas gift." Luna literally beamed with the exciting news.

"I would definitely dub you wise men or women, maybe wise persons. I cannot think of a better gift." Aiden received the single sheet of paper which was far more relevant than the bound pages behind him on his bed.

"It's just a start. We searched several of the newspaper's endless web links for persons who may have had business dealings of any kind with the mayor and then followed a few money trails that we found. That was after first trying to locate the secret accounting books he supposedly has somewhere with no success. Since we're not professional PIs, nor skilled hackers, we unfortunately, lack the ability needed to dig deeper into some of the crime connections of those listed. But there were clearly red flags that made each of those listed on the page a person of interest." Luna admitted.

"Thanks guy, you didn't happen to find any telltale trail of red writing on the wall, did you?" Aiden mumbled.

"What?" Luna looked confused.

"Oh, just a part of the book I was reading. It would be nice to have things spelled out."

"Know these names are off the record and not official, maybe it'd be best to claim they're from an anonymous source. I could lose my job for snooping around unless I could tie them into a sports story somehow, but like Luna said they all have a connection to the mayor on some level. They should give you and your lawyer a start of new places to look for a suspect. It's ridiculous the police have no other leads." Pax was not as big a fan of Birdwhistle as Luna, but fair was fair, and this didn't seem right.

Aiden looked down at the proffered sheet. Less than ten names printed in bold Calibri font were staring back at him and surprisingly he saw the name of Zori's father Marcus

MacQuiod on the list. What the heck, that may explain a few things. He would have to ask Zori about it during her next visit. As soon as he got his computer, perhaps he could do some investigating of his own if Uncle Toby wasn't up to the task.

"Truly you two are the best. I'm lucky to have wrecked my truck near your tree Luna. And Pax you're a great Dr. W."

"Are you experiencing a delayed recurrent concussion?" Pax questioned.

"Or a book reference again. W for Watson, remember? Sherlock's sidekick." Luna puzzled out the strange comment.

"I don't think I'm concussed, just have too much time on my own to think these days and am not sure how I ended up here or if I'll ever get out. Forgive my wandering thoughts."

The two visiting free birds continued to chirp out some inane babble which Aiden was having trouble processing before they departed in the direction that they had come. Their arms were extended around the other's alternate shoulder or waist with smiles stretched across their faces. Aiden sent them off with sincere thanks and his best happy face, despite the melancholy churning in his stomach. His friends could savor their good-deed gift as he lay back down on his non-Christmassy cot. Aiden picked up his new book to continue

150

reading but the words blurred on the page. Murder mysteries were far too real tonight, and he had his own to decipher.

Chapter 15

__The Moon rotates on its axis in around the same length of time it takes to orbit the Earth.__ This means that from the Earth we only ever see around 60% of its surface and 50% at any one time. The side that we can see from Earth is called the near side while the other side is called the far side of the Moon. It is sometimes called the dark side despite the fact that it illuminated by the Sun just as much as the near side. __The phases of the Moon__ are New Moon, Crescent, First Quarter, Waxing Gibbous, Full Moon, Waning Gibbous, Last Quarter, Crescent, and back to New Moon again. A lunar eclipse occurs when the Earth is between the Sun and the Moon.

Luna

Luna and Sherlock were spending Christmas Eve with Pax and Helene Loughty in their residential Moonburg home. Finally fulfilling Pax's offer to stay overnight as a sort of combined Christmas gift to him and a destination getaway for herself. It felt more natural here than being at her parents' home for the holiday and less lonely than staying at the treehouse for solo festivities with her labradoodle. Sherlock was sniffing out his new surroundings but had already done his business outside so should be a good boy, probably just curious about this non-wood, carpeted flooring.

Growing up, winter break between semesters was nearly a month long and had always been her parent's designated time to travel internationally. Mr. and Ms. or Dr. Fernsby, her mother was not a medical doctor but had a Ph.D. in several disciplines, stopped inviting Luna along when she was in college after a trip to Fiji when they determined that "they were required to entertain her and could not just relax and read on the beach". She wondered what far-flung outpost they were off to this year. Luna stopped by their home on her way into town just in case they were there, not really expecting to catch them at home. She left her calling card shoved inside their screen door...a cute little box containing some of her best new tea flavors covered with the Ferns-bee logo. Once again wondering if they were proud of her or found her an oddity and felt that she had wasted her life up to this point. At least her parents had always allowed her space to be herself.

Pax's sister Paisley with her husband and three kids were arriving later Christmas afternoon. Paisley Tumbler wanted to celebrate Christmas morning at her own home so as not to have to pack a passel of presents for the trip which was understandable. Five plane tickets for flights on Christmas Day had been priced at a killer deal. Pax would drop Luna home on his way to the airport to pick up the travelers after the two, or more like three of them had spent Christmas morning together. The Loughty's would get two Christmas celebrations that day. Luna's celebration with them would be their warmup for the real deal.

Or perhaps they viewed inviting her over as a charitable offering at Christmastime. The little tea girl could be reminiscent of the little match girl. The moral of The *Little Match Girl* story by Hans Christian Andersen was after all to behave charitably towards those who are less fortunate. Despite the match girl's dire circumstances, the girl dreamt of warmth and food as she tried to earn money selling her matches. Perhaps that is how the Loughty's saw their little tea girl. That Luna needed a truly warm place to stay as she tried to earn money selling teas from her treehouse. She would try to not overthink the invitation and just appreciate their hospitality. When had she become so unassured? It must be the holiday bubble weaving humanitarian thoughts into her brain.

They had also stopped by the jail on the way to Pax's house. Not to deliver a box of tea bags but a bit of paperwork unearthed from their most recent detective work. Luna was not really sure how helpful their efforts had been, but it made her feel better to keep looking for anything that might create an opening in his defense. Aiden had not seemed as chipper as usual. What was she expecting? If she was more mellow during the holiday season, an incarcerated person must be drowning in the blues. He had acted grateful enough, yet there was a haunting look floating about in his deep blue eyes. Sherlock had been waiting in the SUV or Luna would have liked to stay longer. It was hard to abandon Aiden to an evening alone on Christmas Eve.

Always the homey hostess, Helene Loughty greeted Luna warmly inviting her in. Then immediately started making excuses for the lack of a homemade dinner to serve her.

"I'm sorry I didn't cook tonight Luna. Once it became just me and Pax here on the holidays, we decided to order in ethnic, or perhaps it's more politically correct to say international food, on Christmas Eve each year. We don't travel and get to experience the cuisine where it originated as your family does. Tonight is Japanese. Are you okay with sushi and tempura?"

"Sushi sounds wonderful Helene. I just appreciate you having me here at all."

"And mom makes the best sticky buns for Christmas morning. The dough rises overnight in a bunt pan covered in butterscotch pudding and brown sugar, then we pull the warm rolls apart after they are cooked. They are delicious." Pax raved.

"Again, nothing fancy. I am making a more traditional Christmas dinner for tomorrow afternoon when Paisley's crew arrives. You're welcome to stay and join us." Helene offered.

"Tonight, and tomorrow morning will be more than enough for you to open your home to me, thanks again for including me. I will let the out-of-town Tumbler family have their own time with you two tomorrow. They'll have come a long way." Luna could see that even though Helene's offer seemed sincere, Pax's mom looked relieved that Luna would not be staying for dinner tomorrow too.

It was a good thing Luna had truly been okay with their choice of a Japanese meal because the doorbell rang shortly afterward to reveal a harried delivery boy holding forth two bags of hot food. As Pax took the delicious smelling, hunger-inducing sacks, Mrs. Loughty handed the delivery boy a candy cane with a nice cash tip attached. They were a generous family to whoever crossed their path tonight.

The dining room table was set casually with festive paper plates, plastic eating utensils, and the containers of food emptied from the bags in the middle. The dinner was self-serve family style as they reached for the menu items that appealed most to each of them. Pax went slow until the women had consumed their fill and then cleaned up all the leftovers. He was a big guy, so rice and vegetables were probably not that filling for him. At the end of the meal, all seemed satiated and content as they pushed away from the table.

Helene continued in her hostess mode, "In the past several years there have not been enough of us here to play charades or other group games and when we sang carols, I ended up singing a solo for the most part. So, on Christmas Eve I put out a hot chocolate bar with a choice of toppings to add to your steaming mugs, and then we each choose our favorite Christmas movie to watch and have a mini-movie marathon while we wait for Santa to come. Pax can find almost anything you might want to stream these days."

"That sounds delightful. What are the two of your favorite movies?" Luna asked not wanting to choose the same show or an outlandish one.

"Mom usually picks classics like *It's a Wonderful Life* or *The Miracle on 34th Street*. I have been known to select *The Christmas Story*, you know the one where the boy wants a red rider BB gun, and his mom is afraid that he will shoot his eye out. Or sometimes the irreverent *Christmas Vacation*, but this year I think I'm going for *A Charlie Brown Christmas*."

Luna wondered if Pax's selection was because the Charlie Brown show was safer or much shorter than his past movies. She thought through her mental catalog of Christmas viewing options until she knew what she wanted to see. If she was honest with herself it was by far her favorite Christmas selection.

"If you can find it, I'd like to watch *How the Grinch Stole Christmas*, not the new Jim Carey movie version, but the old original animated Dr. Suess cartoon. I always loved Cindy Lou Who and poor Max the reindeer dog and how the Grinch's heart grew two sizes that day. It is my favorite."

"Sounds like we have our complete viewing list. I'll stick with *It's a Wonderful Life* this year. Pax if you'll get the movies set up, I'll go get the cocoa going."

Luna sat on the couch wrapped in the softest, weighted blanket that she had ever experienced. Helene said she wanted Luna to try out the Minky Couture blanket that Pax had given her last year for her birthday. The soft texture was really something, Luna may never want to leave the lap of luxury she was cocooned in. They each snuggled in to watch the screen with their unique cocoa concoctions.

Helene's cocoa mug sported the traditional candy cane and marshmallows as she took the easy chair leaving the couch for the two of them to share. Pax joined Luna on the sofa with a cup of cocoa so chocked full of every item his mother had laid out that he was going to need a spoon to eat it. Luna was sipping her delicious mug of hot chocolate loaded with crushed Heath bar slivers, a shot of almond flavoring, and topped with a tower of whipped cream. The chocolate tasted especially rich, and decadent compared to her typical cups of tea. One leg was curled underneath her and the other leg hanging down for Sherlock to lean against and feel a part of things. She was not comfortable inviting the dog to sit on the couch with her as she did at home, and he liked to sit on her foot anyway. Pax reached over to wipe an errant smear of whipped cream off Luna's nose. The world felt cozy.

The television screen viewers watched Helene's selection first, since it was the longest, just in case the older woman wanted to head to bed afterward. Luna could not remember seeing *It's a Wonderful Life* before. She enjoyed it immensely wishing everyone had a guardian angel like Clarence in their lives. Then wondered if they did. She would have to remember the angel's reassuring message to George that "no man is a failure who has friends." Next was Pax's tender choice from the *Charlie Brown* sagas, saving Luna's *Grinch* for the end, "the best for last" she declared.

Mrs. Loughty made it through all three shows. Luna kept glancing at Pax wondering what he was thinking throughout their movie marathon. His expression revealed nothing. He was sitting quite close to her but not cuddling. The kiss they had shared when he had dropped her home after their fake date kept coming to her mind. What did she want from him? Pax probably wasn't the kind of guy to make a second move unless she showed some interest herself. It wasn't like her to be so shy, but this was Pax, her main buddy, not her main squeeze. *The Grinch* ended with the whole town in a circle happily holding hands and singing merrily even without any gifts.

Mrs. Loughty gathered the discarded cocoa mugs and carried them into the kitchen.

Pax turned to Luna and asked, "So what'd you think?"

"Nice mix of nostalgia. Truly a lovely evening." She wasn't ready to scoot off to bed and have it end just yet.

"We may not live in a cool tree, but not bad for city dwellers huh? We have an actual big screen and don't have to watch everything on a screen the size of an iPad." Pax grinned so she'd know he was kidding as he brushed a few strands of misbehaving hair off her face so he could look into her eyes better.

"There are pros and cons about most things I suppose." Luna agreed as she spotted something that may prove useful. Standing up, the super-soft blanket slid back onto the couch in an unfolded heap. Sherlock rose and stretched after his long nap as Luna headed towards the stairs. Pax followed behind asking if she was all ready to go up to bed. In their separate rooms, of course, he added awkwardly.

"Nope, I just spotted some seasonal foliage that I don't run into out where I live." Luna stopped under a sprig of mistletoe tacked to the ceiling at the bottom of the staircase wondering if Pax had an idea where this was going. She stepped up onto the bottom stair and waited for him to come to her, then wrapped her arms around his neck drawing him in close.

"I have been waiting for the perfect moment to reciprocate your fake-date kiss when I finally noticed this mistletoe calling me." Luna smiled as she planted a surprise smooch on Pax's chocolatey lips. Worried that Helene might reappear at any minute, Luna kept the kiss short but long enough to express her intent. As she pulled her face away from his, Pax spoke, "Not so fast little lady, I'm not ready for my Christmas kiss to end. I'd like to unwrap it a little longer."

161

"What about your mother?"

"What about my mother? I'm pretty sure she's seen a lot more than kissing even in her old back and white movies." Then Pax whispered softly into Luna's ear, "The scariest thing she would do is break into a solo chorus of *I Saw Mommy Kissing Santa Claus* and I can live with that." With those words, he headed back in for Christmas kiss take two.

Chapter 16

The craters which pockmark the Moon were formed by asteroid impacts from millions of years ago. The craters have not eroded much over the years. The Moon is not geologically very active, so earthquakes, volcanoes, and mountain-building do not alter the landscape as they do on Earth. There are also no weather events, as the Moon has virtually no atmosphere. There is no wind or rain, so very little surface erosion occurs on the Moon.

Birdwhistles and Berrycloths

Meredith or Merri was a Berrycloth before she was a Birdwhistle. Both were good old English names from pre-seventh century England. Born a Berrycloth, she had assumed that her ancestors probably dyed cloth with berries but no, Berrycloth was actually named for a location, a place called Barrowclough near Halifax in West Yorkshire. Locational names were distributed around the country when those who bore the name moved from their original homes and went to live or work in another town or village. Her family had really uprooted and relocated their name. Birdwhistle was not from the obvious either. Nope, not from a man who whittled whistles or possessed a gift for whistling like a bird. Her married name was also locational and related to lost medieval villages in England. Birtwisle, near the town of Padiham in Lancashire; Briestwistle near Dewsbury in Yorkshire; or Breretwisel near Wath-upon-Dearne. The meaning of their name was derived from a fork or junction on a river where birds nest, or a *bridd – twissel.*

Both transplanted families had independently immigrated and lived in Sunlight City before it really was a city, more of an outpost on the mountain. They had hunted, fished, and skied before the tourist industry made it vogue to do so. The Sun Mountain ski resort with its impressive log lodge and high-tech chairlifts were built less than thirty years ago. Merri and her friends had used the rope tow or side stepped up the mountain to get to the top when they wanted to ski down. A few friends had skins they put over their skis that made them able to walk up the hill without slipping backward. Skiing was a real adventure back then. Nowadays she did none of the outdoor pass times that she had participated in growing up. It was a shame really.

William was a wonderful skier. In fact, Merri met him on the slopes. Not swishing down the icy angles but buried in a snowdrift. She had lost one of her ski poles on a rough ungroomed run and careened out of control until she toppled into a cushion of fluffy white. William was not a member of the ski patrol; the group did not exist back then. He had been her rescuing knight that day, not wearing shining armor, but in ski gear and goggles. Merri was smitten from the first gloved hand he extended to help her up. They had skied together the rest of the day and walked side by side every day since.

Only eighteen years old at their fateful meeting, the couple had waited until springtime the following year to marry on the very same slope after the snow had melted. Wildflowers adorned the hills and her hair, adding nature's glorious colors to accent her ivory white dress. William, only two years older at twenty-one, had worn a sky-blue tux the color of his eyes and promised to carry her up or down the mountain, whatever was needed, for the rest of their days and bring sunlight into their lives. Sunlight was the name of their town, but William Birdwhistle had been even more literal creating a solar business that virtually captured the light. They had lived good lives on the mountain near the sun's source. Until recently when their world exploded with Aiden's arrest.

Perhaps they had all flown a little too close to the sun and their son's wings had gotten singed or melted off like the mythical Icarus. Aiden had always been the golden boy. What had happened?

Stoic William kept carrying his load up the hill as if all would be well. That was the only way Willian knew how to deal with trials and grief, just carry on. He was a self-made man who asked little from anyone and took care of things himself. This time the incident might be bigger than he could fix, he could not just pull his son out of the snow. They called for backup in the form of Merri's baby brother, still keeping the assistance in the family. Tobias Berrycloth had supposed expertise in the field that could help save their oldest son.

Merri had been protective of her little brother Tobias since the day he was born. Their parents passed away earlier than most did in these days of modern medicine, and she became as much a mother figure as an older sister to her brother. Toby was like her and William's adopted third son. William had always been willing to support his wife in this venture and agreed to use most of the Berrycloth parent's inheritance for Toby's schooling so that the boy could make his own way in the world with an honorable productive career. There wasn't enough work in the solar business at that time to put an extra on the payroll and provide for two salaries. So,

Toby went to college in Moonburg and barely made it through even with all of their help. He eventually passed his exams but was obviously not fully adept at the field of law. If he had been, their innocent son would not still be sitting behind bars.

Toby struggled in all areas of his life so his lack of success in law should not have been a surprise. There was an excuse for everything. School was hard because he needed glasses and maybe medicine to help him concentrate better, not because he didn't study and wanted to party. His marriage failed because his wife had too high of expectations and wanted things Toby could not provide, not because he had a gambling problem and rarely came home before midnight. William had a good glimpse into Toby's flaws, but Merri was totally blind to them. She was sure her brother was up to the task and would save their Aiden. If they had the resources William would have hired a big shot lawyer from out of town. It was more difficult convincing his wife to select another attorney from the similar bottom-of-the-barrel choices they had to work with.

Rocco watched all the hullabaloo taking place and was just enjoying the ride. It had been hard to make a name for himself in high school. He was not the athlete his brother had been and never seemed to live up to the projections that the coaches and teachers had for him after his brother had set the bar so high. And Rocco was not just talking about the height of the bar over the pole-vaulting pit. Aiden's standard had been set high in all areas. It would have been much easier to follow in his uncle's footsteps. There would have been virtually no expectations and Rocco would have looked like a superstar in comparison.

Now, his talented brother's crown had become tarnished. Rocco could either moan and cry and worry like his mom, ignore it was happening like his dad or ride the celebrity train and get some of his own notoriety out of this whole mess. Rocco loved his big brother and certainly didn't want him to end up in prison or on death row, but they were a long way from that outcome yet. People in high school now knew he existed and cute girls were showering him with sympathy. He wasn't ready for Aiden to be released just yet. Having Uncle Toby in court, the courtroom that is, not on the sports court, was working out in Rocco's favor for now.

The non-incarcerated Birdwhistle three had invited their single Berrycloth relative to join them at their modest home back up the mountain to finish off their Christmas Eve celebration after they returned from the earlier jailhouse visit. Merri had invited her brother over when William refused to have Tobias join them at the jail cell. William wanted their time with Aiden to be festive and not turn into a discussion about the case. Their son needed downtime to forget. Not that forgetting was possible when he was rotting away in jail and not home beside their decorated Christmas tree. Perhaps William was the one wanting to avoid or ignore the obvious.

It was after nine, the stockings were all hung by the chimney with care, but Tobias had yet to arrive.

"I'm going to bed." William announced.

"Couldn't you wait a little longer, I'm sure he will be here soon." Merri pleaded.

In reply, William went over and ripped the Christmas stockings down from where they dangled from the mantel. "This whole holiday is a farse. Why did you even put Aiden's stocking up? It's not likely Santa will be visiting him here." The father of the home strode down the hall to bed without looking back.

Toby arrived not long afterward apologizing that he had to make a stop on the way.

"It's okay, Toby. It's just been a long day," his sister comforted. "I have a plate of food waiting for you in the kitchen. You can heat it up in the microwave. I filled one for both you and Aiden to eat since you two weren't here for dinner. You can sleepover and be here for Christmas morning if you'd like."

"Thanks Mer," Toby headed into the kitchen without telling her where he had been. What could he say? There was really nothing to explain. He didn't even know the truth. He had stopped by the home of an ex. Not for any action as they would probably surmise. And the stopping hadn't taken that long, she hadn't invited him in. It was the shopping beforehand that had taken most of the time. The clerk at the toy store had suggested an American Girl doll saying they were all the rage. Toby didn't think Ella seemed old enough for that kind of doll and wanted one that she could cuddle. He ended up purchasing a baby doll that could cry and wet its diaper and had the store gift wrap it for him.

He wasn't even sure that Ella was his daughter, Toby and her mother had never discussed the possibility. Perhaps his former significant other merely wanted to keep Toby out of the picture. He knew he hadn't been the best boyfriend. However, the timing fit. It was a definite possibility that he had spawned the child. He had just stood there on the porch like a fool with a gift in hand. After an uncomfortable amount of time with no explanation and no invitation to enter, he had offered the package up to his ex, telling her that it was for Ella. Hopefully, she would give it to the girl. What was he expecting? It was Christmas Eve, and he hadn't been invited. Why was he trying to create a family that wasn't his...even if he had donated the sperm? That's all he was at best, a sperm donor. But he was curious if the little girl looked like him or had any of his mannerisms? He was ready to stop running away and settle down.

His sister entered while he was eating and stood over him rubbing his tense shoulders. To her, Toby was still a child, yet he may have one of his own. He needed to step it up in so many areas.

Merri merely felt like sitting in the rocker near the fireplace and crying, but all of the men in her life needed comfort tonight and she was striking out in her attempts to provide it.

Rocco watched his dad finally show some real emotion and then lose control of it. Then witnessed his mom sickeningly coddled Uncle Toby who was nearly old enough to be Rocco's dad. He wished he had gone to the party at his friend's house instead of hanging out at this sh--, he meant crap show. Shoving the door open Rocco went outside to get some fresh air. The sun's warm round orb had been replaced by the lesser, cooler light of an equally round moon. Tonight, hanging out with the man on the moon would be an improvement over his current circumstances. He searched the sky for a Christmas star. One that would be bright enough to guide some wisemen to their location. They were desperately

171

in need of wisdom. The three men in this house, his dad, Uncle Toby nor himself were currently making the cut.

Chapter 17

__The Moon's gravitational force pulls on the Earth's oceans__. The pull causes two bulges of water on the Earth's oceans - one where the ocean waters face the Moon, and the pull is strongest and one where the ocean waters face away from the Moon and the pull is weakest. As Earth rotates underneath, the bulges move around it - one always facing the Moon, the other directly opposite. This is created because gravity pulls Earth toward the Moon more than it pulls at the water. The combined forces of gravity, the Earth's rotation, and other factors usually cause two high tides to two low tides every day.

Moonburg

A nearly full moon shone its light over the city with just wisps of cloud cover swirling across it. The simple beauty of an elegant night sky added to the festive aura even minus the renowned star. Since the original star first appeared centuries ago there had been various alignments of planets sending messages from the heavens. Tonight's sky was clear showering the land dwellers with familiar constellations and galaxies adding their brightness to the strings of twinkling Christmas lights that adorned the city's houses and trees.

Sister city Starville was hosting its annual Star Festival in honor of the famous sky figure of the Christmas season. And Sunlight City was literally a named reflection of the light of the son of God merely replacing the *O* for a *U* in its name...son vs. sun. The citizens of Moonburg had to work harder to find something to squeeze the magic of the season from, yet it was still very much present in the air. Animals may not speak in human languages at the hour of midnight as was fabled to take place, but there was a definite difference in the language spoken on this night. Words came across kinder and gentler backed by expressions of love.

In the hospital laying on a narrow gurney a son in surgical garb prepared to donate a kidney to his mother whose were failing. Other altruistic souls had gathered warm clothes and were preparing a hot meal to serve in the city park to the homeless tomorrow on Christmas Day. In several homes, parents gathered children around hearths below mantles lined with empty stockings to teach them of the most meaningful gifts of the season, the ones that cannot be wrapped and placed under a tree. Tucked away in this cynical world were pockets of goodness wherever one looked if they took the time.

In more sparse circumstances dim light shone on a young man kneeling over a slender metal cot with his head bowed. This location was not the typical place to see such humility. More often its inhabitants railed against all things including their creator. Anger fought against justice within these walls. This oddity cradled within the heart of Moonburg drew no attention on this celebrated night yet should have carved out a hallowed spot within the scope of mankind. If the man on his knees were guilty, he had chosen an interesting place to go for assistance and if innocent hopefully his prayers offered up to a higher power would be heard.

Chapter 18

The effect of gravity is only about one-fifth (17%) as strong on the surface of the Moon compared to the strength of gravity on the surface of the Earth. The Soviet Union's Luna program featured the first successful landing of an unmanned spacecraft on the surface of the Moon in 1966. The USA's NASA Apollo 11 mission in 1969 was the first manned Moon landing. There are only 12 people in the history of mankind who have walked on the moon and all 12 people were from the USA. It started with Neil Armstrong in 1969 as part of the Apollo 11 mission and ended with Gene Cernan in 1972 on the Apollo 17 mission.

Aiden

Christmas morning arose with no fanfare within the jailhouse. There were no stockings filled and its few decorations looked tacky in the daylight. Aiden felt as if he woke with an eggnog hangover though he doubted the drink delivered by his mother contained any alcohol. The heaviness in his head was more likely due to lack of sleep and the plethora of things pressing down on it.

An unlucky guard who must have drawn the short straw to be working Christmas morning arrived with Aiden's breakfast. "Here ya go, fella. Not exactly breakfast fit for a king or even for a Christmas morning I 'spose but some do-gooders did bring by fancier muffins than usual." The officer unlocked the barred metal door and set the tray of food beside Aiden on the bed.

"Thanks, don't suppose I need much nourishment to survive in here. Your meals are better than the bread and water that I always imagined was served in prison." Aiden only half joking graciously accepted the offering placed next to him, then unexpectedly added, "You're welcome to join me if you'd like."

The guard named Silva drew up the stool and took a seat but not too close to the bed, there must be rules on keeping their distance from prisoners. "I thought your baking friend would have you all decked out with amazing grub for today."

"Oh, I'm sure she will be by later today with something. That's the plan anyway." Aiden took a bite of the dry, crumbly cranberry muffin and quickly washed it down with watery orange juice hoping Zori did bring something to eat with a little more flavor later.

"Is she, your girlfriend?" Officer Silva asked.

"You mean Zori? No, not really, I'm not sure what she is or why she comes but I'm grateful. My own personal angel, I suppose." Aiden quipped.

"I'd figure out a way to clip her wings and keep her around if I're you. I've worked here lots of years and even wives of the guys in this joint aren't as devoted as that girl. You've got a good one."

"Yeah, I suppose so." Aiden didn't always feel as lucky as he should. Incarceration did that to a man. "Not sure how to accomplish that unless you lock her up in here with me, not in some creepy conjugal type visit way…," he wished it wasn't too late to suck back in the last odd comment he'd made, finishing with, "…never mind, I'll try."

"Ya know, you seem like an awfully nice guy to get mixed up in this murder stuff. How'd it happen?" The holiday spirit must be fuzzing normal social barriers. There had to be something better to talk about than his arrest.

"Wrong place at the wrong time I guess." It wouldn't do Aiden any good to try to convince a guard of his innocence, he would save it for the jury.

Sensing he wasn't going to get much more out of Aiden, the guard stood, and with a "Merry Christmas" left the cell. Aiden should have been more forthcoming; Silva's company was better than nothing. But nothing or no one was probably better than his next visitor. Tobias Berrycloth stopped by bearing more of the continual non-gifts that he kept on giving.

"Surprised to see you're working on a holiday, uncle." Aiden was not really that shocked knowing Uncle Toby had no one to go home to unless he hired an escort for the day. His marriage had ended after less than a year and his uncle didn't have any current significant others in his life that Aiden was aware of anyway. Aiden would try to cut the guy some slack.

"Doing double duty nephew, part work, but mostly a family visit." Toby told him.

Aiden would hate to see how dismal his visits with non-family clients were, if his uncle had any other clients. "Well, thanks for coming by Uncle Toby. To deliver good news I hope?"

"It depends on how you look at it. The good news could be that you may get less time in here. Although that also gives me less time than I expected to prepare. Your trial has been set to begin at the end of March and continue through the first part of April. It's currently on the calendar from March 24th to April 6th depending on how things go. Three months should give us plenty of time to uncover what we need, if we're going to find anything at all we should by then." Aiden wouldn't have time to complete his Law 101 class by then…and that was the good news?

"So, what's the bad news?" He was almost afraid to ask.

"Well, at this point, the death penalty hasn't yet been withdrawn. Don't worry, I'm still working on that one."

Aiden did worry about it. He could be condemned to death by Easter with only the small consolation that at least crucifixion was no longer an option for execution these days.

"Some friends who have been doing research on their own gave me a list of names to look into for alternate suspects. Has anyone else been interrogated concerning the crime? There have to be others with more or at least as much motive as I do. These friends believe that the mayor was involved in secret business dealings. Do you think there could be a cover-up somewhere in one of the law enforcement departments and that I'm their sacrificial lamb? If so, can we do anything?" Aiden could hear the pleading in his own voice.

"I highly doubt there is some big conspiracy going on and I'm not really a detective, but I can pass along the list of names to one if that makes you feel better." Toby placated.

"What would make me feel better is if my own attorney believed in my innocence and was fighting with all of his might to get me off of these fictitious charges! There isn't much I can do in here for myself. I am trusting you Toby with literally my life."

"Now, now let's not get all worked up. I'm doing my best. And it looks like you're doing okay in here, you've spruced up this place a bit, made it downright homey. Know that if you're convicted, they'll probably move you to the penitentiary in Starville but enjoy it here for now."

That was what Aiden was concerned about, not that he might be moving to another prison, but that his uncle was doing his best and his best was not going to be nearly good enough. He was not ready to resign himself to throwing in the towel and giving up.

His uncle was gone by ten-fifteen. There wasn't much else to talk about after being told you may be put to death. Aiden wasn't tired but laid back down on his cot, he didn't feel like reading and it would be several hours before Zori came by. There must be something better that he could do with his time than lay here and feel sorry for himself. His mind wandered to Christmases past. Maybe the ghost of Marley would come and take him a tour. He thought of the smiling family photos on the Christmas cards that his mom sent out each year wondering what she would say on theirs this season...*It's been a tough year, our oldest son whom we believed had so much potential is wasting away in the county jail on murder charges…*

Then it hit him, he may not be able to go shopping for gifts, but he could make those in his life a Christmas card to celebrate the season. Just thinking about the idea made him feel better. Not seeing a tin mug to drag back and forth across the bars to call his jailer, he shouted loudly hoping to be heard, "OFFICER SILVA."

Silva returned not looking as chipper as he had when he brought Aiden his breakfast tray, "What'd ya want Birdwhistle?"

"Would it be possible for you to bring me some paper and a pen, and maybe some markers if you have them. I'd like to make Christmas cards." Aiden knew it sounded lame, but it was better than sitting in his pity.

"How many pages da ya want?"

Aiden mentally ticked off in his head…mom, dad, Rocco…Luna, Pax, and Zori…six. Then thought he could make cards for Silva and Uncle Toby too. They had attempted to add to his Christmas cheer. "How about eight, no ten, in case I flub up a few times."

"Be right back."

Silva returned shortly with a short stack of computer paper, a ballpoint pen, black and red permanent markers and green, blue and yellow dry erase markers which he handed through the bars without opening the door.

Aiden barely got out a "thanks man" before Silva returned to whatever he had been interrupted doing before the request for card-supplies. Probably cruising his phone for who knows what. Aiden didn't care, he was now equipped. He pulled the stool up next to the bed creating a makeshift desk while sitting on his multipurpose cot for the bench. Folding all the pages in half lengthwise to create the cards, he decided to draw the front cover pictures first, and opened them back up so that the markers wouldn't bleed through onto the half he planned to write his messages on.

Aiden was not an artist, but he could crank out some simple drawings to add color to the cards. First, he used the green marker to outline a simple evergreen tree topped by a yellow star with round red and blue ornaments hanging on it. On the second paper, he made a snowman using the black marker to draw the descending-sized round snowballs, coal eyes, and buttons with a green scarf and blue top hat. The third page sprouted a yellow star. It took a minute to decide if he should draw a six-pointed star of David or the five-pointed one. He ended up making the easier to draw five-sided star filling it in with the yellow marker and adding beams of light shooting out in all directions. He was running out of simple to draw options when he picked up the red marker and made a red and white striped candy-cane. There was no way he had four more unique pieces of artwork in him, so he just drew doubles of the original four.

He would give Luna the tree since she lived in a forest and Zori a candy cane since she always brought him sweets. No, Zori was more the star since she always brought him light. Pax's persona embodied the big round icy snowman and the two extra people he had decided to make cards for would get his worst drawings whatever they were. Aiden added a sheriff's star badge to the lopsided snowman for Silva and that left a candy cane for Uncle Toby if he wanted to give each of his family members a different picture on their cards. Aiden knew it didn't really matter, but he wanted to put thought and effort into his gifts no matter how simple they were. Maybe even more so since they were so insignificant. To give them some meaning.

Now what to write? He just added a brief Christmas sentiment on Silva's and his uncle's. It was more the thought that counted and neither had done so much for him that he needed to write a novel. In his father's he thanked his dad for the good example he'd been and for teaching him to work hard and never give up. His mom may have slacked off since he'd been in jail, but she had been ultra-supportive growing up. He let her know how much all the meals and washed laundry and track meet watching had meant to him. She would probably cry when she read it. Who knew, it could be his last written works to her. In Rocco's card he didn't want to get too mushy so ended it by signing off, "don't do drugs and stay out of jail," then he drew a laughy face emoji so his little brother would know it was a joke since Aiden actually was in jail. Maybe it wasn't funny.

On to the cards for his new friends. Aiden realized that none of the kids he had known in high school had been to visit him. Of course, it had been a few years since graduation, and some may have moved away but still, it was strange. When a person became down and out, they found out who their real friends were. He had a lot more to say to Luna than to Pax and wished he had made them a single card to share, but he didn't know if they were together as a couple or not. Sometimes he got the vibe Luna was still on the market. Aiden finally figured out enough to write about to thank them both separately. He was not creating masterpieces.

He saved Zori's card for last. There was so much he wanted to express to her, yet he could not come up with the right words to say all that was in his heart. Who was this girl and what were their visits all about? They were friends, real friends. He would start there:

Merriest Christmas my new friend. I'm not sure how I scored you but like on the front of this card you have become a star of light in my life. I've even joked that you are my wingless angel. I'm sure it's no coincidence that you come from STARville. ☺ Not sure how I would have survived these last few months without you. There is not much I can do for you in return for all of your trips to visit me, all of the delicious treats you bring me, and just all of the time you spend here. Please know I'm very grateful and will do whatever I can for you too. Obviously, that offer is quite limited these days. If I ever get out, I will be all about paying you back for your kindnesses. For today this juvenile, jail-made Christmas card will have to do. Know you are the best Miss Zoriah ? MacQuiod. (I don't know if you have a middle name). Your biggest fan, Aiden

There, that was the best Aiden could do. He hoped his words weren't too much but just enough to let her know what she meant to him. It was exciting that he would actually have something to give to Zori for once when she dropped by.

Chapter 19

Earth artifacts left on the Moon by astronauts include two golf balls, an obscene Andy Warhol doodle, and a message from Queen Elizabeth II. Eugene Cernan, Apollo 17 commander and one of the last people to walk on the Moon, traced his daughter's initials into the soil when he visited in 1972. Without any wind or weather on the Moon, the letters TDC could remain there forever.

Zori

Zori did not make it to see Aiden until mid-afternoon. Marcus MacQuiod had uncharacteristically planned to spend their Christmas morning together. A catered buffet breakfast with several exotic selections was delivered and set up surrounding a small ice sculpture. There were even fancy fish entrees that made her stomach squirm at the early hour but ended up tasting surprisingly delicious. Her dad was really trying to make the holiday special. The least she could do was participate graciously. The father and daughter took turns opening each of their few gifts individually. The sound of ripping wrapping paper was interspersed with limited conversation. Zori found the whole morning awkward and was restless to get away, but her dad was making such a huge effort she settled into it. He expressed in apparent sincerity that he was concerned about her lately. Well, that concern went both ways.

The most impressive present from her father was a gift card allowing her to pick the car of her choice from the dealership lot. The gift was gigantic, and Zori deeply appreciated it. However, she wasn't sure what models were available off the top of her head. Her dad offered to take her down to the lot right then. Zori promised to go car shopping soon and would ask daddy MacQuiod for his suggestions when she did. Today she had other plans. Zori had given her dad some crazy socks with cars all over them along with a coupon for a weekly personally baked item of his choice. It seemed they did have at least one thing in common. They both liked to give gift cards or coupons.

Having done his Christmas duty, Marcus turned on the television to watch some college football bowl games and didn't ask when Zori left where she needed to go or when she'd be back. That was perfect with her. She hopped into the most recent loaner car she had borrowed off the lot, a boxy

Kia Soul, and sped to Moonburg. The roads were virtually empty on Christmas day and the weather was experiencing a warm snap, so the pavement wasn't icy. She should make good time. Hopefully, Aiden didn't think she had forgotten him. Zori wondered if there were any special activities planned for the inmates on holidays. Not likely.

In less than an hour Zori burst into the jailhouse excited to give Aiden her gift, not the baked goods and buffet leftovers she had brought to share with him, but an Apple Notebook Pro to use for his college classes and whatever else he was allowed to do on it. Aiden had been working on both the permission and finances to get one, but she had pushed both agendas through and planned to surprise him. He greeted her ecstatically with his bright star-covered handmade card and she didn't have the heart to outshine him so slipped the wrapped computer behind her back and would give it later as an afterthought before she left. Truly thrilled about his card, she opened it to read. Aiden suddenly shy, asked her to please wait until after she left to read it. She could do that, silly boy.

There was an unusual barrier between them today that wasn't just caused by the bars. Was he upset she was late? Was it just the heightened emotions of the holiday? Or had something happened? They tip-toed around more meaningful topics of conversation for a while before Aiden opened up with what was on his mind.

"Zori, some friends gave me an unusual gift last night. It was a list of names for me to look into who possibly had unsavory business dealings with Mayor Dankworth." Zori had an idea that she knew where this was going. "Your dad's name is on the list. Could he have possibly been involved with the mayor or his death?"

She should have known this would eventually come up but wasn't sure how to answer. "I must admit that my father does or did do business with Mayor Dankworth. They were friends. I cannot tell you that all of their associations were on the up and up or if my dad is the kind of man who could kill the mayor. I would certainly hope not." Zori really didn't want to talk about this. Not today. So, she switched topics before it got too dark and awful. "I would rather talk about my mother than my father if that's okay."

Aiden looked confused, "Are you trying to tell me that you think your mother may have slipped into town and committed the murder and then vanished again?"

"No, I'm trying to tell you…maybe there is more to my mom's story than my dad's. My mother is dead." It was a special day. Aiden deserved a gift from the heart too and she was about to give him one.

"What? There are two murders now? The fact that I'm locked in here and couldn't have committed the second murder should be helpful. And even more important, I'm super sorry about your loss Zori." Aiden was all over the place now and totally baffled. She needed to clarify.

"When I left you last time. I called my mother again. I call her almost every day. She's my go-to person when I need someone to listen. I told her that would be my last call."

"But why would you do that? Don't you still need your mom? That must have been quite hurtful, was her death a… a suicide?"

"I said it would be up to her if she chose to ever call me back or wanted to communicate. No, her death was not a suicide Aiden. I'm trying to tell you that my mother didn't just die. She's been dead since I was a little girl."

Aiden just listened quietly. Zori could tell that he was battling to understand what she was telling him. Their roles had reversed. She was now the chatty one and not doing a very good job of confessing her heart held secret.

"I'm making a mess of this. Sorry. This is supposed to be a gift to you Aiden…the truth or at least a big part of it. Like I've mentioned, for most of my life, my mother has been my main go-to person. I talk to her every day and tell her everything. Somewhere inside of me, I knew she wasn't there

191

and that she'd never really answered, but I could never admit she was really gone. It was too hard to wrap my mind around. Recently, I realized that I wasn't talking to her every day anymore. Since I've started talking to you, I didn't seem to need my one-sided conversations with my mother so much. I've finally been able to admit to myself for the first time, and now to you, that my mother is gone, really gone, and that she has not just moved away. My parents aren't separated or divorced. Vada MacQuiod died when I was a little girl, and my life has never been the same. There I said it. Now you know that I'm crazy and you might not want me to ever come back."

She could tell Aiden didn't know what to say. It looked as if he wished he could put his arms through the bars to hug her and then decided to try. Zori moved as close to the metal barrier as she could and let Aiden pull her even closer to him. His cheek pressed against hers in spite of the cold bar trying to keep them apart. Possibly the wisest words she had ever heard spoken flowed from his mouth. "It's okay Zori. Grief is just love with no place to go."

On her drive home those words kept repeating themselves in her brain…grief is just love with no place to go. And she wondered if a boy from the sun and a girl from a star fall in love where do they live? Must they settle for the moon?

CITY THREE

Starville

For some unfortunate reason, swamplands seem to drudge up a negative connotation. There can be beauty in darkness. I embrace and ingest the grit, grime, and coloring-outside-the-lines of my existence. The environment brushed around me could be an interpretation of the famous Starry Night painting personified. Vincent van Gogh's piece of art depicted the original view from an east-facing window of his asylum room at Saint-Rémy-de-Provence just before sunrise, with the addition of an imaginary village that could easily have been me. Starville may not be as idyllic as the imaginary village portrayed but it does capture a touch of the asylum aspect from van Gogh's work.

It's interesting that the dimmest and most crime-ridden city in this solar circle is called by a name of light. Albeit stars are the heavenly bodies that exude the least light, nonetheless, there's still a drizzle of light emitted. Looking up into a star-strewn sky is majestic. I like to think of myself from that perspective…star-strewn not dim or lacking in any way.

Many people move here to hide from the world and to do things that are best done in the darkness of night, undercover, hidden. My overlying color day or night and the accompanying atmosphere are best described as gray. The residents' skin even takes on a touch of the grayish tone after a few years. Buildings themselves aren't built in the swamp but are surrounded by marshy uninhabited land where nefarious activities often take place, making my boundaries an ideal location for the prison. Inmates didn't have to change their residential expectations much to board behind bars as most had bars on their apartment windows on the outside anyway. The penitentiary is just another dreary home away from their former dreary home for many who enter. This one with regular meals.

Gambling, embezzling, drug dealing, the porn industry, and murder are common within my boundaries. It should bother me I suppose, but I've gotten used to it. Corruption breeds corruption.

There are edifices of learning, but not many students graduate, the dropout rate is high. While academics may not be on fire, our sports teams do incredibly well. Not that they're extremely physically fit, but they know how to play dirty. Win at all costs is the essence of the breed that lives in these lowlands.

Clouds of smoke hover over my midtown to south town areas due to the high number of factories and industry. We crank out all sorts of production with few environmental standards. Some of the goods can be considered worthwhile, like the solar panels for a Sunlight City solar business. Others are just to make money and could be relocated to improve the air quality. Profit is the bottom line in these parts.

The attitudes of those that dwell here are less than cheery but not many move away. My city somehow has a holding force that keeps its citizens and families here for generation after generation. Mayor Dankworth represented his constituents well. He let me grow naturally to become what I was meant to be without city planning or sprawl control. With morally flexible businessmen like Marcus MacQuiod things should remain status-quo for quite some time. His daughter Zoriah is a bit of a rabble-rouser but as in most locations, the majority rules.

I suppose some may measure me less desirable than my sister cities in various categories, although I do surpass them in a few areas. My real estate is the least expensive. My population is not less than theirs, in fact, I have more residents than pretty Sunlight City. Moonburg may have more educated citizens, but Starville is brimming with street smarts if I do say so myself. No one has to put on airs and pretend to be something they're not in my district. Members of the human race are not all looking for identical things when they settle down. Junkyard dogs hold their own in a fight. We may come away with a few scrapes and bruises but will cling onto the prize. My economy is booming, and I'll trade a tourist for a shrewd businessman any day. There are no stars in my eyes, but I can see plenty in my future.

Chapter 20

"Twinkle, twinkle, little star..." **is a real song, but stars don't actually twinkle.** *As the light of a star travels into our realm of vision turbulence in Earth's atmosphere cause disturbances in the light's path, creating the illusion that a star is twinkling. There are billions of stars in our solar system, but at best, on a very clear night and far away from any light sources, you might be able to see some 2,500 stars.*

Zori

Zori only told Aiden part of her truth on Christmas Day. Not only was her mother actually dead, but her middle name was Celeste, and she hadn't meant to kill the man. Exactly the opposite, she had gone bearing gifts. The murder could be viewed as her father's fault, not that he'd made her do it, but he had created the association that had caused the horrific state of affairs. Mayor Dankworth had a hard job and spent a lot of extra time working with her dad, so Zori had prepared a baked offering designated especially for him. That morning she had arisen a few hours before she needed to be at the dealership and tried out a new breakfast cupcake recipe. It landed in the mixed culinary category somewhere between a cupcake, coffeecake, and pastry. She had added fruit filling and drizzled a glaze across the top. Then taken off to make the delivery to the mayor's office while the confectionary was still warm. Hoping to surprise the mayor, instead, she had surprised herself.

The lights to the mayor's office appeared to be on when she walked by his window, so she decided to leave the breakfast treat on his desk with a little note or perhaps anonymously, she hadn't yet decided. Cracking open the office door to deposit her baked goods she heard the mayor speaking. No one appeared to be in the room with him; the conversation was taking place over a cell phone. Mayor Dankworth's pattern of speech was much rougher and more unprofessional than she had ever heard it during their previous encounters. He seemed to be quite upset about a few kids that had been left in a van outside his office. Zori didn't even know the mayor had kids, but his conversation sounded like a domestic dispute. She had obviously arrived at an inopportune time and was about to make a hasty retreat when the mayor pulled open the door apparently on his way out as well.

The shock splashed across his reddened face had been obvious. "Miss MacQuiod what are you doing here?" The mayor's voice had softened and sounded quite different than it had on the call, "How much of my conversation did you just hear?"

Zori had been flustered, if she had been thinking clearly, she would have said nothing, that she had heard absolutely nothing. Hindsight always has much more clarity. Instead, she had blurted out, "Not much, just that your kids are in the van. Sorry, I'll let you go to them. You can share these breakfast cakes with them if they're hungry. I just wanted to thank you for all you do."

That last line seemed ironic now. Mayor Dankworth had grabbed the cupcakes along with the girl holding them and pulled both back into his office shutting the door behind them. At that point, an eerie feeling had crept all the way up her spine and megaphone level alerts instructing her to leave immediately screamed in her head.

"You can keep the cakes, but I should probably take off for work. I'm on foot so it will take me extra time and I hate to be late." Yes, that should explain it. She needed to go, now.

"Not so fast little lady. Let's have a word before you go. Those kids aren't mine. I have nothing to do with kids. Do you understand?"

"Sorry I just thought…"

"Don't think, okay. I need to think. This is a real mess. First, the dumb driver left the kids here instead of where they were supposed to be delivered and now you. I doubt you can keep your mouth shut." The mayor was still holding onto her upper arm with a very tight probably bruise producing grip.

"Oh, I'm a great mouth keeper-shutter. I'm an only child and my dad works all the time. I really don't have anyone to talk to. Mums the word." Zori wasn't even sure what she was being mum about but locked her lips and threw away the imaginary key with her free hand.

"Really, because you seem like a damn jabber-box to me. I think you need to go for a ride with the kids. Not my first plan. Marcus can never know."

What could Marcus never know and where were the kids going?! Zori doubted it was to the zoo. "Thanks for the offer, but I really should be getting on my way."

"What you don't understand missy is that this isn't an invitation. It's a command. You're cute enough and they'll love your white hair and pale eyes. A fresh one, even if a little older than they like. I'll try to make it up to Marcus somehow. It's too bad that he lost his wife too.

Realization was dawning in Zori's mind. The mayor planned to take her away and all she had wanted to do was give him breakfast cupcakes. The kids in the van outside weren't his, but they were going to the same place he planned to take her. If wherever they were headed *'liked them younger than her and fresh'* Zori was starting to get the big picture. She had heard about sex trafficking but never imagined it might be happening this close to home. If she went with Mayor Dankworth, she realized that she would not be going home, probably ever. It didn't sound like the mayor planned to kill her, she wouldn't be dead like her mother, the death that she had not been able to acknowledge for years. But what the mayor planned to do with her would kill something inside of her that was even worse, she would never be the same. She might as well be dead.

Mayor Dankworth still gripped her arm tightly, probably trying to decide how to get her out the door without Zori creating a scene. He was bigger and stronger than she was. He was also older, slower, and out of shape. Zori was not an aggressive girl, but she felt her adrenaline start to kick in. She was not going to go quietly to the van without putting up some kind of a fight. The image of the butter knife that she had slipped into her jacket pocket to touch up the breakfast cake's icing if any got smudged on the way here came into her mind. The flat-edged knife was not much of a weapon, but it was better than nothing.

With her free hand Zori grabbed ahold of the handle on the thicker end of the stainless-steel knife, pulling the unimposing armament from her pocket she began stabbing it at the mayor's chest.

Laughter erupted from Mayor Dankworth's mouth, "You're a feisty one for sure. That attribute is often appreciated by your future clientele."

Zori was now fully enraged. Who did this man think he was? Zori was pretty sure that the form before her was possessed of pure evil. Her knife jabs were making no headway cutting through layers of dense clothing, she doubted they had even scratched the surface of his skin. Before the mayor could take her away, Zori's only hope was to find a place that the dull weapon could do some damage. She scanned his body. Only the mayor's hands and head were bare. Hands were too quick and an injury there wouldn't slow him down enough, but the face was a possible target. Eyeballs were especially vulnerable, but that was so gruesome. Zori didn't think she could purposely blind a person.

She cocked her arm back to give the blow more force. Mayor Dankworth was taller than she remembered. Zori doubted she could reach his eye with any real strength and there was so much bone on the face that she would never be able to penetrate if she missed. On her forward thrust, the metal tip of the knife found its own entrance place. Just below the jawline into the softness of the mayor's neck. The silver blade slid easily below the surface of the skin and sunk deep. The mayor's eyes which she had spared from damage opened wide in instant shock and pain. What had she done?

Blood in mass quantities began to drain from the wound and stain his white collar before dripping down onto the rest of him. The mayor let go of Zori and reached for his neck to remove the knife. Before he could grasp and pull it out, he fell to his knees too weak to finish the act. This looked much worse than Zori had planned. She just wanted to get away from the man.

"Stupid girl. What have you done?" Mayor Dankworth spoke in a shrill whisper. He was no longer on his knees. He had fallen backward seated on the floor with his back slumped against the desk. The piece of furniture was the only thing holding him up.

"I didn't mean to." That wasn't really true. Zori had meant to injure him, perhaps not this badly.

"You have killed me." The blood was no longer only covering the mayor's hands and clothes it was pooling onto the carpet on the floor. Zori must have hit a major artery. Her aim was not that good. In her frenzy there had been no designated target. Destiny must have guided the innocuous weapon.

She panicked. There was not much time to decide what to do. The mayor was fading fast. Calling 911 was not going to be much help at this point. Her breakfast cakes were resting on the desk where the mayor had set them as obvious as any business card in pointing out her presence.

"I'm sorry, sir. Truly. I came to do something nice for you and you had other plans for me. Sometimes things just happen. I believe it's called karma." Zori was not sure if the mayor could still hear her. He was lying flat on the ground now or as flat as he was going to get. A calm coldness spread through her, and Zori realized that she must be going into shock. Resisting the urge to straighten the mayor out and make him look more comfortable, Zori grabbed the offending frosted breakfast muffins. They had caused this terrible event. Some crumbs slid from the plate onto the mayor's desktop, but Zori didn't take the time to clean them up. Instead, she pulled a few tissues from the Kleenex box on the desk and wrapping them around the handle on the knife pulled it from the mayor's neck. What must be the last drops of blood left in his body drained from the stab mark. Sickness filled her stomach threatening to erupt onto the floor and mingle with the fluid already there. She supposed she could have just wiped her fingerprints off the knife, but it was too late. This murder weapon would never be used to frost another of her cakes, but it could not be left here.

Clutching the cupcakes, she fled from the scene not sure if anyone had seen her or not. Out front, Zori saw the non-descript white van that the mayor must have been speaking about. She could not leave the children trapped inside of it to suffer the same fate that he had planned for her. The mayor obviously had an accomplice, probably the person who had been on the other end of the phone call, and they would be coming back before long. Luckily one of the front doors had been left unlocked. Zori climbed into the cargo van and saw that there was a partition between the front seats and whatever was in the back. The kids must be contained in that back section. A long thin window above the bench seat allowed her to peek into the darker space, but it was too narrow to pull out the three terrified children trapped there. They were smaller than she was but not small enough. However, the space was big enough for specially baked breakfast cupcakes to fit through.

Sounding more normal and much more cheerful than she felt, Zori spoke to the cowering kids. "Good morning cuties, I can imagine that you haven't been having the best time in this van. I've brought you some breakfast and will get you out of here soon." Zori held the paper plate with four muffins through the opening. The children didn't move. Of course, they probably trusted no one at this point. "It's okay. I promise. I'm sure you must be hungry."

Slowly one of the three children, who appeared to be a young boy, crawled forward taking the food from her and returned to share it with the other captives. That should keep them occupied for a few minutes while she figured out how to free them before anyone else arrived. Zori searched under seats and in the glove compartment for a key to open the back doors. The original driver must have left it with the vehicle for the mayor to get the kids out when he arrived or take them to wherever they were going. She could try to pry the back doors open with her handy, multipurpose butter knife but that seemed macabre. The bloody weapon needed to stay hidden in her pocket if possible.

Rifling through the paperwork in the jockey box, she found what she was looking for. A set of car keys imprinted with the Dodge logo. Through the opening, Zori shouted,

"I've got the key," before hurrying around back to open the double doors and free the little ones.

"Can any of you find your way home from here or get to somewhere safe?" She asked the frightened youths who were shielding their eyes from the brighter light outside the van. The boy who had accepted the food nodded his head in affirmation and was gone before she could say more. The other two children were girls that appeared far more hesitant. It did not look like they wanted to leave their rescuer. Zori needed to get out of here like right now and she could not drag them along with a fleeing fugitive.

"Listen, you can use my phone to make a phone call, or there is a police station two blocks down this street where you can get help. I'm sure there are people who love you looking for both of you and I really need to go."

The slightly taller girl who was likely the older of the two offered, "We can go to the police station." She looked slightly suspicious of Zori and did not take the proffered phone.

"I would take you there myself if I could. Please hurry and get out of this area as fast as you can." It was still early. The girls were of an age that they should currently be in school and would stand out like a blinking neon sign that they did not belong in this part of town. The two ran off on their spindly legs holding each other's hands. Zori called after them, "The station is on the right just past the intersection after you cross the next street. Be safe!" The smaller girl waved her hand over her head back at Zori as they took off. Zori would check up on them later from a distance to make sure they arrived safely but not close enough that she would be indicated in their escape and possibly fingered for the crime that initiated it. Kid's statements could be confusing.

A large yellow truck with a logo written across the side pulled into the parking space on the opposite side of the van. Zori could see a man about her age behind the steering wheel and she did not want him to see her or be able to identify her later to the police. Ducking her head to hide her face, Zori headed in the opposite direction from the one that the two girls had run, she went back towards MacQuiod Motors. She would wash the knife off and disinfect it when she got there. Then put it into the silverware drawer in the break room. No one would look for a murder weapon in there. Her idea had worked, for the last few months employees of her father had been eating their meals with it.

If Zori knew then what she knew now she would have handled the whole thing differently. She should have not gone in the first place, but she did free the kids. Perhaps she could have baked poison into the breakfast cakes that day instead. It would have been far less messy, and poison was not a method traditionally used by men so Aiden would not likely have been arrested. Poison may have been misdiagnosed as a heart attack or some other natural cause. The mayor was definitely not in tip-top condition. However, she had no idea going there that dreadful morning that Mayor Dankworth was a demon in disguise. The act was not premeditated. And how could she have gotten him to eat the baked treat before dragging her off to the van? Insist that human trafficking is a taxing activity, and he needed some nutrition before starting off. Not that her baked items were especially nutritious. Then who knows who may have eaten the rest of the cupcakes on the plate. There could have been more accidental deaths. No, it was just an unfortunate chain of events and she would do the same thing again if pressed. If she hadn't, those kids would still be in the van or in a place far worse. Turning herself in had not crossed her mind as an option.

Zori had shared none of this with Aiden. No one knew. She never assumed the guy in the yellow truck would be accused of the crime that she committed. When he had been arrested, she was sure that he would get off soon. How could Aiden not be acquitted; he had not committed the crime. The longer he stayed behind bars the more she worried. She did not want Aiden to be convicted of a crime that she had done.

If things didn't start to look better for him soon, Zori would speak to Aiden about escaping. And if it looked like he would be prosecuted for the murder, maybe they could run away together and find a place outside of their scenic loop solar system where they could live together happily ever after.

Chapter 21

An average star is between one and ten billion years old, although some stars are much older than this. The most massive stars live shorter lives compared to smaller stars because large stars burn through their fuel much faster. Giant stars explode into a bright supernova when they die. The most common type of star is a red dwarf. These stars are less than half of our sun's mass and size. Red dwarfs burn very slowly, extending their lifespan to over 100 billion years. These stars shine less than others because they are cooler and as they age, they get dimmer until they disappear. Unlike giant stars, such as supergiants and hypergiants, small red dwarf stars do not explode.

Aiden

Aiden mulled over Zori's unexpected confession about her mother. The woman was actually dead and had not merely left their family and moved away to a distant location as he had been led to believe. Well, if he untangled it myopically, heaven was the most distant move that he could think of and was definitely a place difficult to visit if you wanted a return trip. History only told of one person who had been able to achieve that feat. Aiden didn't believe Zori was mentally ill, it was more that she had used a child's way of coping with an event that she could not process in any other manner. Her self-preserving defense mechanisms had kicked in. The girl was unique in many ways. Aiden had become accustomed to having her around, he even looked forward to her visits and expected them. He leaned on her. That was a self-preserving act of his own. He did not want to spend his life alone in prison or lose it over an act he did not do.

He wondered if a plea bargain was still on the table. Perhaps he should reconsider that option if it wasn't too late. Aiden believed with all of his heart that he would be found innocent. He had also believed that he would be freed by now, so he wasn't so sure if his beliefs were spot-on accurate these days. It was hard to see things clearly when one's view was limited within four windowless walls. It was time to talk to his uncle again.

Aiden decided to work on his Law 101 assignments until his uncle arrived. Perhaps it would get him into a legal frame of mind, and he might even uncover something helpful that they could use in his defense. He was working on the computer that Zori gave him for Christmas. It was an extravagant gift and made him feel a little awkward after only giving her a card. She did take good care of him. Internet use in prisons allowed inmates to communicate with the outside world and opened their horizons. However much like the use of mobile phones in prison, internet access without supervision, via a smartphone, was banned for all inmates. So, Silva or whoever happened to be on guard duty had to be hovering nearby and making random checks on his screen. It's not like he was searching how to plan a breakout, looking at porn or doing anything inappropriate. The supervision was slightly embarrassing but worth it.

His first law course was designed "to help students develop elementary skills in legal analysis". Aiden was well beyond needing rudimentary skills, a master's level knowledge would be beneficial right now. Topics he studied included: the structure of the legal system, analysis of rule creation and rule application jurisprudence, and legal argument. The knowledge he needed to take the online tests could be gained from assigned readings, cases, lectures, and in-class exercises. Only one of those was an option for Aiden unless the lecture was broadcast online. His professor had been kind enough to present his class lectures over Zoom as well as in the classroom so that Aiden was able to take part. The opportunity gave Aiden a glimpse outside his cell-bound boundaries stimulating his mind beyond the four dreary walls. Zori's suggestion to take college classes had been inspired.

After finishing his basic assignment for the day, Aiden decided to delve into some extra reading on case studies which the title of the article claimed where *Cases Every Law Student Should Know About*. Skipping down the page until he found a few that dealt with murder cases, Aiden read first about a case called *R v Dudley and Stephens*. It determined that necessity wasn't always an adequate defense against murder.

In 1884, on the 5th of July, Tom Dudley, Edwin Stephens, Edmund Brooks, and Richard Parker were shipwrecked and adrift in a lifeboat seven hundred miles from the nearest land with no fresh water and only two tins of turnips to eat. By July 17th, they had eaten the turnips and the entirety of a turtle they had managed to catch, and by the 24th of July, Parker had slipped into a coma. Realizing that there was no other way to survive, Dudley and Stephens killed Parker, and the three remaining men, including Brooks, resorted to cannibalism in order to survive. On the 29th of July, they were rescued.

When the case was brought to trial, public opinion was highly sympathetic to Dudley and Stephens, to the extent that their defense was paid for by public opinion. At the same time, the judiciary wanted it established that necessity was not a defense for murder. The ultimate outcome of the case was something of a compromise. Dudley and Stephens were convicted of murder but sentenced to just six months in prison.

That verdict was hopeful, such a short sentence for murder and cannibalism. Aiden hadn't taken even one bite out of Mayor Dankworth upon finding him dead. Since the first case was encouraging, Aiden decided to read one more about a college student around his age.

The *R v Rabey* case took place in Canada more recently in 1980. Wayne Rabey was a twenty-year-old geology student who was romantically interested in a female classmate. So far, it sounded much like normal university life, that is if the person were not in prison. However, when they were studying together, Rabey found a letter the girl had written to a friend of hers where she said that Rabey "bugged" her, and described him as "nothing", also mentioning that she was interested in someone else. When Rabey met her in the corridor later that day, he asked her what she thought of him. She told him she saw him as a friend, and he attacked her and hit her with a rock sample that as a geology student he happened to have in his possession.

At the trial, he claimed that he had suffered such a psychological blow that he had slipped into a state of automatism, but that this was a one-time occurrence and wasn't likely to happen again; that it was "non-insane automatism". The court held, and later the Supreme Court agreed following an appeal, that if he had entered a dissociative state, this was "insane automatism" requiring psychological treatment and non-insane automatism wouldn't count as a defense. The verdict was presumably a relief to fellow geology students everywhere, but Aiden wasn't sure he could use automatism, whether insane or not in his defense.

Cases were still swirling in Aiden's head when Tobias Berrycloth arrived at the jail a little later that day with a whole new aura about him. Aiden wasn't sure what it was, but the man no longer appeared drenched in defeat and there was a lilt to his uncle's step.

"Good morning nephew." And for some reason the comment sounded sincere, it did feel like a good day to Aiden. "I was able to interview both of the deceased's ex-wives and many of the people on the list you gave me." Aiden's observation was correct, his uncle was not himself today, he had actually done some useful leg work on the case.

Toby continued, "Neither of the women had anything good to say about Dankworth but I didn't get murderous vibes from them either. His first wife has been divorced from him for seventeen years, she has grown kids and seems to have moved on. She could care less about the man or his death. His second ex admitted that she thought Dankworth was a total scum bag and wanted nothing to do with him. However, she made the valid point that she would have preferred to keep the man alive, he was worth more to her alive than dead from an alimony standpoint. She suggested that I should talk to the mistress. Definitely some unresolved issues there. Dankworth doesn't sound like a standup guy, yet even he had better luck with the women that I've had. It's incredible." His uncle was attempting humor.

"I also spoke with some of the others on your list. Didn't get any major leads but I'll call a few of them to the stand during the trial and see where it goes when they're in the hot seat. Sometimes unexpected things slip out under pressure."

"D'you think any of them might have done it, you know killed the mayor?"

"Well, none were exactly admirers, but they all had pretty airtight alibis."

What had the man in front of Aiden done with his uncle? Had there been an alien abduction or a body-snatching exchange? Aiden was actually impressed for once. "Were you able to talk to Mr. MacQuiod? I get the feeling that he may have been involved somehow?"

"Not yet, he's been slippery. I did speak to the District Attorney and asked if he would have their detectives and prosecutors interview those on the list you gave me. They'll have more leverage and backing than I do as an independent. We'll see if they can get Marcus MacQuiod in."

His related-by-blood attorney had stepped up his game or was now at least on the playing field. Something had lit a fire under his uncle. Aiden's earlier thoughts of plea bargaining flew out of the unreachable window. There was still time to fight. "Do you want to put me on the stand?"

"Maybe. You're a likable all-American type guy. The right jury with of a lot of middle-aged white women would want to bring you home, some of them to their own homes." Toby chuckled at his trial humor; he was in a chipper mood. "Of course, some juries could eat you alive. It'll be a crapshoot, but I'm leaning towards yes. Put you in that clean-cut suit with a good haircut and your megawatt smile. You'll melt enough hearts that hopefully they'll have trouble putting you away behind bars for the rest of your life."

The strategy was sounding better. Aiden may not end up as a *case every law student should know about*, but at least it sounded like they had some kind of case and that was an improvement.

The positive energy continued to flow later that day when Zori showed up with a cake shaped like a mini ski mountain covered in coconut flakes with a tiny ski figurine perched upon it.

"I thought you might be missing your ski mountain this season." Zori explained.

"So, you brought me a mountain that I can literally experience on another level… internally. I can taste my skiing from the inside out." A smile spread across Aiden face.

"It's great to see you in a happier mood." Zori noticed, "Although any mood is understandable in here," she quickly added.

"Yup, I actually had a decent meeting with Uncle Toby today. Things are looking slightly up. He's talked to some alternate suspects. There are actually a few out there and you may know some of 'em. And he also mentioned that they'd probably be moving me to the longer-term facility in Starville if I'm convicted. I thought you'd be interested in that update."

Zori did seem interested and a little rattled by the news. "Let's hope your move is out of here, but not to another prison. In the worst-case scenario, you'd be closer to me in Starville and I could visit every day. Of course, it would be best if you were cleared and freed, but if not, I'll be there."

Then casually added as if an afterthought, "Oh, and who are the other possible suspects?"

"I guess it is premature to say anything. They're just names of persons who could have reason to be involved with the mayor or wish him harm. I will tell you that your father's name is on the list."

"I guess I'm not surprised." Zori almost appeared relieved if that was possible. He must be reading her wrong. "My dad did do business with the mayor as you know, and I guess we never know what a person is capable of when pressed."

It seemed like a strange response from a daughter, but Zori was an unusual girl and her relationship with her mother was anything but normal so why should the one with her father be any different. "I just feel like I have a shot now. I may not spend the rest of my life here or in Starville's prison."

"You may not have to no matter what the outcome of the trial. Have you considered escaping if things don't go well? I'd help plan it. We could run off together somewhere where no one would ever find us. I'm not sure where that place is yet. Obviously not to hide out at my mom's now that we both know the truth."

Was Zori joking or serious? Aiden was not really sure but would assume the former. Planning to break out of prison was not really in either of their skill sets that they would list on a resume. He was getting far too reliant on Zori. Did he have a convict crush or was he using her? Would any warm body that showed him attention these days do, or could he imagine a future and life with Zori in it? Did he even want to? One day would he have a house full of nearly albino babies who looked just like their mother or would she remain the president of his nonexistent fan club bringing him daily baked wares to the Starville prison? Inner conflicts raged within Aiden. He hoped to hold onto the positive direction that his life had taken a turn towards today and keep the ever-encroaching darkness lingering beside him at bay.

Chapter 22

When a person looks up at the night sky with their naked eye all of the stars appear to be the same color, but in actuality, they are not. Stars have different colors depending on their temperature. The hottest stars are blue, followed by white, yellow, orange, red, and the coolest stars are brown. This can be confusing because we associate red with hot and blue with cold. Heated objects change colors as they get hotter, a glowing red object is hot, but it represents the lowest heat seen under light. As something gets hotter it changes to white and then blue.

Berrycloths and Birdwhistles

Tobias Berrycloth decided that he would ask Ella's mother for a paternity test. Not for the benefit of his ex, but for the small girl who may be their combined DNA daughter. The decision felt right and flooded him with relief. If Ella was his daughter, he wanted to become more involved in the girl's life, and even if she wasn't, he wouldn't mind playing a part in it. However, her mother might find that scenario weird, so Toby wanted to stake a legal claim on the girl. He was pretty sure that she was his. As a lawyer, he had easy access to procure a court order for the paternity test if needed. The requests usually originated from the mother of a child who was often seeking child support, but there was no law that said a possible father could not initiate one.

Toby had tossed around the idea of attempting to collect a secret DNA paternity test which just required a sample from each person, usually a mouth swab from the father, and a discreet sample from the child, the mother's DNA was sometimes gathered but not necessary. Although several sample choice options were acceptable, if he used a strand of hair for the DNA test, he would have to make sure that the hair's root was still attached as the shaft of the hair alone will not do. That snatch could prove more difficult. A range of other DNA samples could be used besides a hair strand including bloodstains, toothbrushes and nail clippings to determine his paternity. Each of these options sounded totally creepy even to himself, so Toby had decided to be honest with his ex and just ask outright for the test.

Awkwardly standing on her front porch again, Toby knocked on Ella and her mother Mandy's door with the paternity test in hand. The female face that opened the door looked less than welcoming.

"What do you want now Toby? Thank you for the doll, Ella loves it, but you don't need to keep coming by."

Holding out the kit, without explanation, Toby stated the obvious, "I want to come by."

"What is this? Another gift?"

"Not exactly. I'd like to get to know Ella and play a more permanent role in her life if she's mine. It's a paternity test. She just needs to swab the inside of her cheek. Or we can get a legal test done with court admissible results if you're willing. This one is mostly for your peace of mind."

The professionally gathered DNA collection cost more than triple this home test kit. The cost didn't matter if it enabled Toby to become a father. However, the at-home test was nearly 100% accurate and used the same genetic markers to determine kinship as the tests performed by law enforcement agencies so even if he had to do both, this one would give him a pretty positive idea of where he stood for now. Toby just wanted to get his foot in the parenthood door and be able to be a part of his maybe-daughter's life if possible.

"You've got to be kidding. I'm not sure I want you to be a part of Ella's life. Did you notice that I never requested a sample from you to determine your paternity? We're doing just fine."

"I understand, I do. I was a jerk. Just give me another chance. I was a flub up before, but things would be different. I promise." Then realizing she may think he wanted to start their relationship back up added, "I know you'll have other men in your life at some point, perhaps even now, I just want to be a constant for Ella if she's mine. I won't go away or ever leave her."

The demeanor of Ella's matriarchal guardian softened, "Leave it here and I'll think about it."

"If you do it now, it'll be done, I'll leave, and we can know the results in two to five days. Then Ella can have an official father in her life. Your participation with me is totally optional." That last line did not come out at all the way he had wanted it to. To counterbalance the verbal mishap, Toby gave his ex his best effort at humbly pleading eyes to show her that he was a repentant man. Sorely aware that his skills with women were woefully limited. "I'm not going anywhere."

Mandy took the DNA test from him telling Toby to remain on the porch and that she would be back before too long. In over ten but less than fifteen minutes his ex and the possible mother of his child returned with the collected sample. A darling little towhead-blonde girl with curly locks past her shoulders and bright blue eyes peered from behind her mother's hip. It looked like there may be some Berrycloth genes hiding in her. In five days or less Toby would know if he were a daddy. It may not be the way most fathers found out about their new bouncing baby boy or girl, but he would take it.

At the Birdwhistle abode marital issues were beginning to crop up between Merri and William. The two, like most couples, had endured rough patches before and were well aware that most successful marriages took work, but it was as if a permanent wall was being built brick by brick between them. Merri worried that William would never forgive her if Aiden was convicted of the mayor's murder because her brother had been unable to free him from the charges. William was bucking his own feelings of guilt for not being able to provide well enough for his family that he was able to afford the legal counsel they needed for their son. The Birdwhistle house already had a second mortgage on it to cover their business costs, the business didn't have enough equity to get a line of credit and their credit cards were maxed out at the lending limits. William knew his behaviors came across as if he were mad at Merri when actually he was more upset with himself. His pride blocked the way into his wife's arms along with the opportunity to transverse this terrible journey together. Healing was much more difficult when not a dual effort.

Recently, Rocco's high school world was not as blissful either. More often than not, his ride on the celebrity train was interrupted with unexpected jolts of ridicule and taunting. Not from the soft-hearted girls who would still occasionally show him some comfort, but from jealous, meathead bullies who either had nothing better to do or wanted in on the unsolicited female attention. Today his charming fellow classmates with the unfortunate names, Beckin Relish and Lemmy Villin, happened to be his designated tormentors. On most days Rocco could ignore any unwanted words tossed his way, usually by pretending he had not even heard them. Today, he was either finally fed up or worried enough about his brother's impending trial that he lost his nonchalant edge.

"Hey, you, brother of Aiden the Ripper or is it Birdwhistle Bundy come on over here. We want to talk to you." One of the two losers, it sounded more like Lemmy, hollered at Rocco. At first, Rocco just kept on walking. Then Lemmy's partner in crime chimed in.

"Aren't you being a little tough on the guy, his brother's only committed one murder so far, he's not a serial killer yet,". Rocco stopped walking.

"That we know of Beck, there could be bodies hidden all over this county that start popping up at any time," the antagonist counterpart continued.

Fury began to fill Rocco's whole body. He forced his words out through clenched teeth, "Have either of you ever heard the saying innocent until proven guilty?"

"Oh, looks like the proofs there, little brother. From what we've heard Sunlight's golden boy has gone dark."

And that was enough. Rocco had had it. With that last derogatory comment hurtled against his big brother, Rocco's rage erupted and bubbled over. He knew there were two of them, but Rocco had enough angry adrenaline to attack a room full of bodies if necessary.

Slowly turning around Rocco surveyed his surroundings. Seconds stood still. No one else was really watching or close enough to get involved or stop him. With all of the force that his non-athletic body possessed Rocco rushed forward throwing his full body weight against Lemmy using every ounce of pent-up emotion that he had been suppressing for months. They fell to the floor together, the back of Lemmy's head thudding onto the scuffed linoleum as Rocco started plummeting his oppressor's face with alternating fists. Blood spurted from Lemmy's nose. At this point, Beck got into the action sending a few sharp kicks into

Rocco's side before grabbing ahold of Rocco's shoulders and pulling the Robo-bot punching machine off of his downed companion.

Rocco's fists were still swinging but connecting only with air. He whirled around landing some blows into Beck's soft stomach as enemy number two yanked him up. It didn't take long for Mr. Beckin Relish to let go of Rocco's shoulders and start landing some punches of his own. Rocco didn't feel a thing. His pain was dulled by the explosion of the male hormones swirling under his skin. These blows were not only for Aiden but for all of the anguish this whole awful event had caused their entire family.

The next opponent's punch met the side of Rocco's head knocking into it the realization that this blow would leave a mark and he'd probably have a black eye in the morning. With a return jab, his knuckles connected with Beck's teeth, and Rocco hoped that he had just knocked the tooth loose and not broken it. His parents didn't need more bills to stress over. The fact that Rocco's fight at school and the frame of mind that caused the fisticuffs might be more concerning to them than their bills never entered his revenge-filled head.

By now, Lemmy was beginning to arise from the initial surprise attack. Rocco knew he could not keep both boys off of him for much longer, but he would fight to his dying breath if it came to that…feasibly, it wouldn't. He could only bob and weave for so long unloading an occasional good strike before they would finally corner him. It didn't take a strategic genius to figure out those odds.

A crowd had begun to gather. Most cheering for the underdog, only a few sided with the demonic duo. Eventually, a math teacher emerged from the nearest classroom shouting above the din of the students for all three to halt and cease their battle. Rocco was far from ready to stop even with the knowledge buried somewhere deep within, where hidden reason dwells, that the teacher's intervention was rescuing him from a complete pummeling.

"Lucky for you Birdwhiste," Lemmy still taunted with blood dripping from his nose onto the front of his shirt.

"Yeah, good thing you have a lawyer in the family, you're going to need it." Beck joined in. "Maybe you can get a two for one special on the cell next to your brother."

Rocco didn't say a word. He didn't need to. His fists had done enough talking.

"Let's take a trip to see the principal shall we," the math teacher whose name Rocco did not know instructed them. "We'll let him get in touch with your parents and sort this all out."

Breathing deeply, the battered fighters followed the instructor turned referee down the hallway. Just what Merri and William needed, one more problem son to worry about.

Chapter 23

Our Solar System resides within the Milky Way galaxy. When the skies are dark and clear the Milky Way appears like a bright belt of stars. Its age is estimated at a whopping 13.2 billion years old and it contains an estimated 100-400 billion stars, but these numbers are constantly changing as new stars are born and old stars die out. There are no pictures showing the entire scope of the Milky Way since the Earth sits inside of it. A person would have to leave our own solar system to capture a picture of the entire galaxy.

Pax

Pax was working at the newspaper office after spending a full eight-hour day working at the bank. He was finishing up an article for tomorrow's paper on a basketball game that he had just watched. Not many hard copies were printed off these days since subscriptions were down, but online readers would want to know the box scores and highlights of the local high school game. Basketball was not his favorite sport to cover, though it might be the easiest due to the lesser number of players on the court to keep track of. Basketball had far fewer players than football did, and the games finished in less than two hours unlike unending wrestling matches and track meets that could go on for three or four.

He didn't actually have to come into the office to submit the article. His presence there was mostly to cover past unwarranted trips into the building when he had come for personal reasons. Pax was nervous that his employer may find out and not be thrilled about the extra-curricular online researching he and Luna had participated in using the newspaper's vast-reaching network equipment. He had not heard a word so far. Junior sports writers must not be on the radar of their higher-ups.

Writing sports articles was not the best job, but Pax actually enjoyed it more than his banking gig. He really needed to decide what he wanted to be when he grew up. It had been years since he wanted to be a policeman, firefighter, or superhero. There must be a job out there that would still inspire him. Perhaps he could be a marketer for Luna's tea business. He had the skills to do marketing. His banking background gave him insights into small businesses and the newspaper job added some advertising skills. With all of her creative energy, Luna was great at making the teas. However, she did not do as well at or even enjoy, her attempts to sell them. The two of them might make a good team. If her business was going to thrive and grow it needed to start branching out at some point. He could be in on the ground floor as one of her first branches. The imagery seemed blatantly fitting for a business built and run in a treehouse. Pax would like to be in on the ground floor in other areas of their relationship as well.

He and Luna had traveled back to Starville another time on an additional sleuthing errand, and they hung out on most Saturdays, but they had not shared another kiss since Christmas. Luna hadn't initiated one and Pax didn't want to run her off if she wasn't really interested in him *that way*. Paisley had given him a hard time when she was home over the holidays about his hesitance to make a move on a girl who was clearly interested in him, but Pax was not so convinced. Paisley hadn't seen them together. Luna did not give off any I'm-crazy-about-you vibes to him, but perhaps he didn't speak that language.

Pax's relationship designation appeared to be more in the realm of Luna's sidekick. He tagged along with her to see Aiden regularly. What was it about a man behind bars that brought out bleeding hearts in some women? The inmate didn't even have to be that handsome, though Birdwhistle was a good-looking guy, not that Pax noticed. When leaving Moonburg's jail last time, they had passed another girl going in to visit Birdwhistle. His female admirers were going to have to take a number soon since jail visitations were limited. If Birdwhistle was found innocent or acquitted Pax could have real competition on his hands. Perhaps it was time to do something about his inaction. What was the worst thing Luna could do? Well, the worst thing would be if he made things so awkward that she never wanted to see him again.

He wrapped up the article he was writing but instead of heading back to his mom's, Pax took the highway north leading out of town. Either his car had a mind of its own or he was about to do what he had wanted to for years.

Luckily, Luna was still up. Pax didn't want to scare her with an unexpected visitor when the sun was nearly down. She appeared happy to see him, but puzzlement was also written across her face. She probably assumed he must be bringing bad news like someone had died or something. Sherlock ran over as Pax opened the SUV door and greeted him with a big wet kiss. Why wasn't it that easy with women? A guy knew exactly where they stood when welcomed with wet kisses.

"Hey Pax, what's up?" Luna called down, before following her dog towards the vehicle.

"Nothing really, just had a hankering to see you." Wow, could he be any lamer?

"Oh, okay. D'you want to come up or just talk down there?"

Luna didn't sound convinced with his explanation and Pax didn't want to be trapped in her treehouse if things went south. "It's a nice night, out here's fine. I won't stay long."

Luna pulled a couple of her outdoor chairs closer to the firepit in case it got chilly. "Well, then take a seat, my friend." Things were not off to a good start if she was already addressing him as *friend*.

"Yeah, about that, I'm honored to be your friend and all..." Pax could see Luna's eyes begin to fill with apprehension in anticipation of the dreaded relationship talk but he plowed on. Seeing concern was better than seeing her eyes glazing over in boredom, at least there was some kind of emotion going on. "...but I'm ready to be more than friends." Luna's eyes got wider, she looked frozen in place still staring at him expectantly, so he continued. He may as well go for broke. "Luna, will you marry me?"

The words just popped out with no preparation like they could not be contained any longer. He could have started by asking her if she would sleep with him, but his feelings for Luna went beyond that. Unfortunately, he had failed to bring a ring to accompany the impromptu offer in the long shot that she actually said yes. There was a beer in his car, his finishing-the-article reward that he had yet to drink. Pax was pretty sure it had a ring-type pull tab on the can. The liquid courage in the can, or two or three of them, would feel nice about now or at least dull the pain of Luna's likely rejection. But how could he in good conscious give a tea girl a beer can ring? That would not only be tacky, but it also verged on blasphemous. Pax quickly scanned the area to see if there was anything from nature he could grab as a substitute fill-in ring replacement until he could get an official one. The distraction was less awkward than looking directly into Luna's face since his embarrassment and increasing horror were building in the length of time that Luna was taking to answer.

Finally, out of her perfect lips came not an answer, but the question, "Are you serious?" Not the first response any man dreams of from the woman they love after asking for their hand in marriage. Even if the proposal was given without previous discussion or warning and caught them totally off guard. Then, probably realizing Pax was indeed serious when he didn't respond in his typical lighthearted manner and not wanting to hurt his feelings, Luna added, "Can I think about it?"

At least it was not a "no". Pax could slink away in defeat but that was not his style, so he offered her a simple, "Sure," and attempted to change the subject. "Do you want me to build a fire? We could make some smores." Nope, Luna needed to explain herself, there was a lot more going on in her head than Pax could obviously comprehend, and she wanted to clarify. This was going to be painful.

"It's not about you Pax. I'm just not sure I want to leave the life I've made for myself out here. And although your mother is truly a lovely woman, I couldn't see myself comfortable constrained in another woman's house, under her supervision and rule, even Helene's.

"I get it." Duh, what twenty-first-century woman wanted to live with their mother-in-law unless they were from far east Asia even if his mom was perfectly okay with the arrangement. Pax was more than ready to change the subject now, where were smores fixings when one needed them, it appeared he has opened a can of worms instead.

"The more I think about it though, there would be some nice parts about having a partner to go through life with." Luna hadn't mentioned the said partner by name, perhaps any partner would do. Would she rather live with him somewhere than stay in her treehouse alone forever? "I can give you something more definite when you come on the weekend. Sorry."

"No, sorry to surprise you," Pax apologized. "Having you as a friend is better than nothing, I'm good." Although Pax was very far away from good at the moment.

"What if we could live in my treehouse on weekends at least?" Luna suggested as she plowed on with the marriage proposal train of thought not letting it pass. Pax could not believe what he was hearing, a glimmer of hope had entered the discussion even if head-over-heels enthusiasm was absent.

"Actually, I found a condo on the edge of town that could be our own place, something for weekdays if you're seriously considering it. I thought we could keep your treehouse for your business as well as weekend escapes from the city." Not the romantic event he had envisioned, his proposal had become more of a negotiation, but marriages were often a work in progress. Luna was not a typical girl. She had run her own unusual realm for as long he'd known her. If he was waiting for her to react exactly as he expected and wanted her to, he might lose her.

"That might work." And with that tiny acquiescence, Luna threw him an impish smile.

Fueled by hope, Pax unabashedly leaped to his feet at the 'perhaps' of the response and easily swept Luna off of hers. All of the missed kisses he had been holding on his lips for a decade exploded forth and were splattered abundantly over Luna's laughing face and down her soft neck. Geez, these were more like Sherlock's slobbering kisses than those of a fiancé. Drawing back for a breath, Pax tenderly laid his mouth upon Luna's and gave her a kiss worth all of the others combined. She was his home no matter where they lived.

Chapter 24

__The Sun is the closest star to Earth.__ It takes light from our Sun 8.2 minutes to reach the Earth, however, it would take around 19 years on a Boeing 747 to reach the Sun from Earth. Most stars, except for those in binary star systems, prefer to live in solitude. If a person were to float around outer space, they would find only single stars shining solo with very long distances between.

Luna

Luna decided to ride her bike into Moonburg for a solo trip. Spring was in full bloom and she reveled in the beauty of the fresh green world erupting all around her as she pedaled. Wildflowers dotted the landscape. Even the air smelt new and inviting. Luna hoped she would be as beautiful a bride as mother earth in all her rebirth glory. She wondered if she should pick up a bridal magazine when in town, she was clueless about the duties of a bride.

The main reason for her trip today was to stop by and catch her mother on campus during Dr. Fernby's office hours to let her know the exciting news. Optimistically, her only daughter's wedding should be exciting news to her mother since her parents comprised all of Luna's official family. Her mother had never pushed her to have a conventional relationship, perhaps Dr. Fernsby would find traditional marriage archaic. Luna didn't really care. Her mother had married. Luna was happy with her decision and needed to share the fact that she was getting married with someone besides Sherlock.

She pedaled up to the social sciences building and left her bike out front beside the cement stairs leading to the wide double doors. Her Roadmaster Granite Peak mountain bike didn't have a lock. Luna had no need for one at the treehouse. It was a budget bike and had obviously been heavily used indicated by the wear and tear displayed. She doubted any of the college students would ride off with it. If one did, perhaps they needed it more than she did. However, she would miss the old girl if it disappeared. Its textured tires made cruising on both rough cobblestone and smooth city streets easy, even riding through the tough terrain in the mountains was a breeze. Her bike had become a trusted friend.

Dr. Mom seemed surprised to see Luna encroaching upon her collegiate world, but with a gesture of the hand offered her daughter a seat in the chair across the wide desk.

"What brings you here today Luna? How is the tea business going?"

"My visit has nothing to do with tea mother, I just wanted to let you know I'm getting married." Luna blurted out.

There was no rush of emotion or congratulations, her mother was a woman of business. "I assume the intended groom is Mr. Pax Loughty unless you have a secret admirer that I am unaware of. When will the event take place and what will be my responsibilities?" Her mother cut to the chase while turning the corners of her mouth up in an appropriate way to show pleasure.

"Nothing mother, I just want you to come and be happy for me. We don't have a date yet, probably this summer so we can hold it outside."

"If you're not going to have it in a chapel or an event center, the campus grounds are a perfect place for an outdoor wedding." Dr. Fernsby suggested.

"That's true, but I'd prefer having it at the treehouse."

"Luna, certainly, you cannot host a formal affair out in the woods. Where will you entertain your guests, what if they need to use a restroom?"

"It will be a small group mom, and that's my happiest place. I want it to have it there." Luna was not going to let her

243

mother bulldoze her about her own wedding. She wanted her parents to attend but not set the tone of the beginning of her new life together with Pax.

"I can address your invitations in calligraphy pen during slow office hours if you'd like."

"Thank you, but that won't be necessary. We'll probably just have our families there."

"Well, what else is there…your dress, flowers, photos, food? What do you need from me?"

"Pax plans to give me a wedding bouquet and I'll just use wildflowers if we need any other flora décor. We talked about using a photographer that Pax knows at the newspaper to capture a few photos. The guy works the same games Pax covers and Pax also plans to host a dinner at his favorite restaurant the night before."

"Sounds like you two have things in hand and don't really need a mother of the bride." Luna was not sure if her mother was relieved or miffed by the comment.

"You could help me find a simple wedding dress or some kind of outfit that would work if you have the time mother, I'm not a big shopper as you know. And I'd love a small wedding cake with some kind of appetizers, or light food spread for the wedding event itself. Something besides my go-to smores around the campfire would be nice. You have such classy taste mother that I'd appreciate having you involved. Oh, and maybe you can tell dad for me."

"You should tell your father, but I'd be delighted to help with your dress and the food."

Luna knew delighted was just the correct word to use in her mother's social science education, but she would take it. "Thanks, mom, I'd like that, and of course I should tell dad myself." He would be easier to tell than her mother anyway and he'd probably show more empathically supportive emotion. Her father was the more emotionally attuned of the two if Luna were holding a competition. But neither parent was likely to cry at her wedding.

Having completed all she had set out to do, Luna said her hug-less goodbyes and exited the walls of academia happy to find her Roadmaster bike laying in the grass against the stairs waiting for her. She thought telling her mother would make the whole wedding thing seem more real, but Luna still felt like she was in a fairytale fog. She could not believe she was actually getting married. Not ready to pedal back uphill she decided to drop by the jail and visit Aiden without Pax for once. She hadn't spoken alone with him since he showed up at her treehouse months ago. She could share her recent news or just see how he was doing. Perhaps telling him about getting married was not something that would cheer him up when his future was yet to be determined.

Aiden had his head down working on a large jigsaw puzzle when she arrived.

"Hey, push that card table over near the bars and I'll get in on some puzzling action with you while we talk." Luna announced upon her arrival.

His blonde head lifted from the puzzle to register she was there, "Sure thing Luna, glad you're here." But the glad in his words did not extend to his eyes. She could sense that Aiden was struggling.

Aiden pushed the table against the barred wall allowing Luna to reach through and add a puzzle piece. "What are we building here? It looks like you got more furniture."

"Another friend of mine dropped off this puzzle of the world, it's the globe flattened, along with a table to build it on so I wouldn't have to use the floor. It's definitely too big for the stool. She thought it'd help me to see beyond these bars and plan what to do when I get out. Forward thinking I suppose."

"How's that working for you?"

"It does help fill the time, but I cannot seem to get my mind off the trial next week. I can't believe it's real. That I might actually be convicted of murder. It's like living in bizarro world."

"Life can be surreal alright." Luna agreed as she fit into place a piece of South Africa.

"I'm so dang keyed up. I can barely sleep. The unknown is so unnerving."

Luna didn't feel like it was the time to share her happy impending nuptials news. It'd be like… "I know you're facing life in prison or even death, but I'm getting married so let's talk about that." If Aiden noticed the engagement ring and asked, she would fill him in. Slipping it off of her finger now would draw more attention to its presence. Pax had put the simple vine embellished band with small emerald stone onto her right-hand ring finger on the visit following his unprepared proposal. Without even having her help pick it out, the ring was utterly perfect. "I'll be there at the trial if you'd like."

"Thanks, any moral support I can get would be wonderful. Maybe seeing that I actually have friends in the courtroom will help convince the jury that I'm not such an awful guy." Aiden was working on the northern hemisphere and slipped a piece of Norway into place as he spoke.

"Norway would be a nice place to visit." Luna acknowledged the country that Aiden had just completed.

"Yeah, I'd rather be over there than in here, even in the winter when it is probably just one big freaking icicle." Aiden answered with a weak grin. "Pretty much any place but here would be nice right now." Maybe the puzzle was working.

They had patched together much of Asia and part of the Indian Ocean with the notched cardboard pieces before being interrupted by a newcomer's voice coming down the hallway. No one else ever visited when Luna was here with Pax. She had rarely seen anyone else in his area, not even other inmates.

"The officer said you only had one guest, so he let me come back too." An extremely pale girl with the lightest eyes Luna had ever seen joined them. A stab of something unpleasant hit Luna in the gut. Was she jealous? She was recently engaged and totally happy with Pax so that made no sense. What was this emotion? Maybe as an only child, she had never learned to share her toys which translated to sharing her good dead causes as an adult. Aiden was hers to help. He had shown up at her treehouse. The new girl felt like an interloper.

Aiden must have picked up on the added chill in the already cold room. "Luna this is Zori, the giver of the puzzle with a table to construct it on, Zori meet Luna." Aiden ever the gentleman politely introduced the two women.

The look in Zori's eyes was as cool as their color. Daggers shot from them. Yes, this was what jealousy looked like. "Nice to meet another *friend* of Aiden's." Luna clarified.

"It's hard to believe my two favorite female visitors have never officially met before." Aiden's comment was certainly meant as a compliment, a man would not realize that the comparison could only serve to increase the level of competition between the two. Zori continued to look leerily at Luna as Luna reached for another piece of the puzzle. She had finally located the specific piece she had been searching for and snapped it into place with a perfect fit.

"The puzzle is a great idea by the way. I'm leaving most of it for Aiden to do but thought I fill in a few pieces while I'm here." The ring on Luna's right hand was very visible as she picked up another tiny piece. Zori noticing its significance seemed to soften.

"Are you married?" She asked.

"Not yet, I just got engaged."

"What, the big guy locked you down?" Aiden asked with a touch of surprise in his voice. "Sorry. Bad choice of words, but good for the two of you. Not that I know much about it, but I can guarantee marriage is nothing like being literally locked in a jail."

Both girls laughed at his jailhouse humor. If Pax wasn't in the picture would Luna have been interested in Aiden? He would certainly be a catch if not imprisoned. But no, he was several years her junior and she doubted he saw her as romantic material anyway. Pax was comfortable. He was her guy. She would be happy to be his bride. The best marriages were supposedly built on friendships and they had that in spades. There was a definite spark in the chemistry department between them as well. But just because she had ordered didn't mean she couldn't check out the man menu occasionally. She would leave now and let Zori have time alone with her intended prey.

"Guess I'll see you at the trial next week Zori. Try to talk this guy off the cliff will you. He's a bit stressed." Luna shared.

"Sounds like you'll have a great rooting section, Aiden. We can even bring signs with *Free Aiden* written on them, or I can pass out baked goods to all of the jury on your behalf." Zori joked.

"She could probably even make your wedding cake Luna; Zori is quite the talented baker. You should've seen some of the bad boys she brought me in here." Then glancing over at Zori added quickly, "Sorry I didn't ask you first before offering Zori, incarceration must be affecting my manners."

"No, that's totally okay, a wedding cake would be a fun challenge if Luna wants me to."

"When we get that far, a cake would be great, but let's get through this trial first." Luna suggested. Pretty sure that her mother would be totally fine just doing the other food for the wedding minus the cake.

"Thanks, ladies. You're both the best. I'd never get through this mess without you." Aiden sounded super sincere. Luna could not imagine how it would feel to not know what the future held. Perhaps no one really did. She was sort of in that situation, but her uncertainty dealt with a happily ever after outcome. Aiden was truly facing life or death in the hands of a jury.

Chapter 25

It takes millions of years for a star's light to reach our eyes, meaning we are seeing stars from long ago. Looking at the night sky is like looking back in time 100,000 years. On a clear night, a person can see as far as 19 quadrillion miles up into the sky. Deneb in Cygnus is a bright start that can be seen in fall and winter, it is 19 quadrillion miles away.

Aiden

Aiden sat behind the defense table waiting for his uncle to arrive. On the inside, he was a tangle of severed nerve endings but on the outside, he looked composed. Immaculately groomed to a spiffy appearance he was the image of a model citizen. His hair had been cut and styled by a professional hairdresser that Uncle Toby had received permission to bring into the jail. The suit selected for him was a slim-fit cut and accentuated his athletic physique nicely. He had been coached to appear sad but to occasionally flash his

All-American smile, only at appropriate moments of course, just so the jury could get a glimpse of his leading-man face. Aiden hoped he was ready. It was the most important day of his life. How could Uncle Toby be late?

Shortly, Tobias Berrycloth slid into the chair beside his nephew breathing heavily like he'd been running. "Sorry, I'm late. I just got back the results. I'm going to be a father."

Even though Aiden was slightly miffed with his uncle this was big news, so he gave him a pass. Wondering who the baby momma was, he asked a safer question instead, "Congrats Uncle, when's the baby due?"

"Oh, she's four years old. Her name's Ella." And with that question-inducing answer, his uncle ended the baby conversation and switched into full-on attorney mode. Aiden's day of reconning had arrived.

The jury entered the courtroom single file and took their assigned seats. His uncle had informed him that there would be seven women and five men on his jury. If Aiden was on trial for killing a woman instead of a man, Tobias would have switched the ratio and gone for more men. In case the individual jurors identified and sympathized more with victims of their own gender. The group appeared to be a wide range of ages and ethnicities. It was about as diverse a representation as could be gathered in this remote area.

Last week the defense and prosecution had selected this jury during a *voir dire*. At the question-and-answer session, Toby had not had to dismiss any jurors due to the fact they were related to or acquainted with anyone involved in the case... the deceased, the defendant, or one of the lawyers. Each lawyer could request the dismissal of an unlimited number of jurors for cause. Toby had explained to Aiden that a challenge for cause occurred when a request to dismiss a potential juror was based on a specific and stated reason. Lawyer Berrycloth had only sent five possible jurors packing.

The first one he sent home was a woman who lacked relevant life experiences, she seemed far too sheltered and would likely be shocked by any kind of crime let alone a murder. Then one of the younger men had to go too because he appeared to be easily influenced by social pressure if his over-the-top trendy attire and incessant phone checking were any indications. The third admitted to having read much online about the case and gave the impression they had already decided that Aiden was guilty. The fourth was far too comfortable with the death penalty and the last was rejected because Aiden's uncle feared he wouldn't be able to be impartial. An out-of-state family member had been murdered recently and the killer not found. This person may subconsciously seek retribution in this trial for the missing suspect that they had no control over. Toby assured Aiden this group of jurors was the best he could come up with from those available. The twelve should be fairly objective without potential or actual bias.

In advance of the trial, Uncle Toby had also requested of the court a motion in *limine* which allowed all key evidence in question to be decided upon beforehand without the jury present. He hoped in doing so to prevent any surprise evidence showing up unexpectedly during the trial and preclude the jury from ever learning of any disputed evidence. His uncle had been much more on the ball than Aiden ever thought possible. Becoming a father appeared to have made Tobias Berrycloth more responsible in other areas of his life as well. His parents had to be pleased. Aiden was thrilled. This trial may not end up being a trapped turkey shoot after all.

A tall, portly bailiff called the court to order and everyone in the courtroom arose as Honorable Judge Augustus Trousseau entered taking his place behind the bench. His impassive dark face and darting black eyes hovered above his black robes and whatever lay beneath them like a magic eight ball floating upon a fortune teller's cloth-covered table.

"Ladies and gentlemen of the jury, the proceedings will be the criminal case of *Mr. Aiden Birdwhistle vs. the State*

255

in the murder trial of Mayor Daniel P. Dankworth. Everyone may be seated. Are all lawyers ready to proceed?" Heads at both the prosecution and defense tables nodded. "We will hear each of your opening statements following which the bailiff will swear in the witnesses for the prosecution."

The lead attorney for the prosecution began with their opening. His well-prepared statement provided an outline of the case that the prosecutors expected to prove. Because neither side wanted to look foolish to the jury, they were careful to promise only what they thought they could deliver. Their team's main points centered around the investigation's inability to uncover any other suspects for the murder, the defendant's opportunity, motive, and fingerprints on the body itself. Wrapping up with the evidence that they planned to present and the issues the jury would need to decide.

In some cases, the defense attorney reserves their opening statement until the beginning of the defense case. Uncle Toby went a step further, he chose not to give an opening statement at all. He wanted to emphasize to the jury was that it was the prosecution's burden to do the convincing. His client was innocent until proven guilty. Aiden sure hoped the twelve picked up on the subtlety. His life was one the line here. He braced himself for the prosecution's witnesses.

Each witness was sworn in by the bailiff to tell the truth before the judge asked each of them to state their name then instructed the attorneys to begin their examination. The prosecution began to present its main case through the direct examination of their witnesses which lasted most of the morning and throughout the afternoon.

Mayor Dankworth's secretary was again the first to be called to the stand. Her most incriminating comments were that "no one else was scheduled to meet with the mayor that morning before he was found dead." Like a murderer would make an appointment Aiden thought and hoped Toby would point out the ludicrousness of that statement. She also added, "Mr. Birdwhistle had been extremely upset when he called for an appointment."

His uncle didn't use the word ludicrous but did throw out some valid cross-examination points. Attorney for the defense Berrycloth asked, "Aren't many people upset about some issue when they come to see the mayor? And did you actually see Mr. Birdwhistle that morning? He has stated that he did not see you."

The mayor's administrative assistant, as the court found out she preferred to be called, became a bit rattled and admitted. "I may have stepped out for a moment to pick up my morning coffee, but I didn't need to actually see Mr.

Birdwhistle to know he had been there." Tally a point for the Tobster.

Next to take the stand was an eyewitness who stated that he had seen Aiden in his truck the morning in question driving away from the county building where the mayor worked in quite a rush. The actual words used by the witness painted an even more vivid description exclaiming that "the guy took off like a bat out of hell". Tobias ignored the hyperbole and aptly pointed out in his cross that the witness's testimony was merely circumstantial evidence. "Mr. Birdwhistle has admitted that he was there that morning and of course he was distressed from finding the mayor dead. Nothing the witness has stated actually proves that Aiden committed the crime." Aiden would call that round a draw. The witness did put him at the scene.

A customer of Sunlight Solar who must have been either upset about his bill or the service he received testified under oath that he had heard Aiden complain that the mayor was "killing" their business. His takeaway was that Aiden may have felt justified in killing the man due to his angry disposition and comment. Uncle Toby countered by asking the solar customer if he had ever used a word that was exaggerated or not exactly what he meant. The witness claiming lack of memory of such an experience refused to answer. Sunlight Solar may need to screen its customers for possible antagonists in the future.

The judge called for an hour lunch break and returned to his quarters. Toby had pe-ordered take-out Subway sandwiches delivered for the two of them to eat at the defense table while they went over what had transpired so far that morning. Both of them felt fairly encouraged. Aiden turned around a few times to see his family and friends seated in the chairs behind them for support. During the morning testimonies he had seen his mother wiping her eyes with a handkerchief, once his dad had given him a you-got-this' look, and Rocco sported a thumb's up. With a mouth full of Italian sub, he swiveled his neck to look over his shoulder again. Luna, sitting alone, offered him a mega-watt smile. Pax must be at work. Zori was on the opposite side of the courtroom across from Luna sitting partially hidden behind his family. He tried a few times but couldn't catch her eye. She did not look up at him at all but appeared to be looking down at her hands. The hoopla was probably stressful for such a non-social girl. In here she couldn't pass around her baked treats to diffuse direct attention.

After lunch, a few random witnesses including two women and one man, that the defense did not even bother to cross-examine, took the stand. Their backup testimonies offered nothing really new to the discussion and nothing specifically condemning, so Toby let these witnesses off the stand without a cross-examination. Then the prosecution called their final witness of the day.

A very official looking forensic expert stepped forward. Aiden noticed the jury watching him with interest. Whatever this man said they were bound to believe. The prosecution directed question after question the expert's way, each was answered calmly with expertise.

Plaintiff's question, "Does any evidence place the defendant at the scene?"

Forensic expert, "Yes, Mr. Birdwhistle's fingerprints were found on the body and in other places around the room."

Plaintiff question, "Does anything else link him to the crime?"

Forensic expert, "I would say that the force in which the murder weapon was thrust into the victim's neck indicated it had to be applied by someone quite strong or fueled by extreme amounts of adrenaline due to the excessive loss of blood occurring so rapidly. Mr. Birdwhistle is a muscular, athletic man. He definitely fits the loose specifications of the person who committed this crime."

And they ping-ponged back and forth, the prosecutor sallying a question and the forensic expert returning a convincing answer. The professional witness threw around like confetti impressive-sounding terms of several forensic pathology techniques that they had employed in solving the crime…physical and fingerprint matching, hair and fiber analysis, blood spatter, or in this case flow and DNA analysis. There had been no need for ballistic analysis as a gun had not been used. The jury was eating it up and buying into every word. Aiden wished the defense team had their own expert witness to impress the jurors.

Uncle Toby staunched some of the bleeding by pointing out, "Mr. Birdwhistle admits he was at the scene. He was willing and attempted to perform CPR, but it was too late. And he is not the only strong person who knew or had issues with Mayor Dankworth." But much damage had already been done. Day one ended with a professional's opinion confirming that the evidence pointed to the fact that Aiden did or at least could have committed the crime. The prosecution finished presenting its case leaving a blanket of doom draped over Aiden and a metallic taste in his mouth. Tomorrow would be their turn.

################################

Aiden did not sleep much if at all. The faces of each of his family members, along with those of his friends and each witness on the stand danced through his brain all night long.

The morning dawned sunny for springtime with a whisp of clouds breaking up the soft yellow rays. Rain was in the forecast. Hopefully, it would be just a light sprinkling from the spring sky and not a deluge flooding darkness into the courtroom. They needed all the light they could get in there.

Uncle Toby informed Aiden that the defense had an option to move for dismissal of his charges if they thought the prosecution had failed to produce enough evidence to support a guilty verdict. Toby didn't think they were there quite yet, but they could try. The judge almost always denied the defense's motion to dismiss, but Tobias wanted to keep Aiden informed and involved in his own defense. Aiden's mind wandered wondering if he would be able to apply for some college credit for a legal internship working on his own defense. He doubted if anyone else on trial had thought of inquiring about it before, but it wasn't a bad idea. That way, win or lose he'd get something out of the experience. His mind returned its focus onto his uncle just in time to hear that they were not going to move for dismissal.

It was their turn; the defense was up to bat. Time to present their main case through direct examination of the defense witnesses. He and Toby had argued about putting Luna on the stand. Toby insisted that Luna had no actual evidence that Aiden hadn't committed the crime apart from his word. Aiden felt strongly that her testimony was important since she was the first person to see him after the event happened. Luna had discovered him in a state of shock and heard from his very own lips that he didn't commit the crime and witnessed that he was willing to turn himself in. Toby gave in to Aiden's debate; Luna was just finishing up her testimony. She did extremely well, turning out to be quite rational and believable for a person living in a tree.

Then the plaintiff pelted her with their cross. "Why didn't Mr. Birdwhistle turn himself in to the authorities immediately? Why did he flee the scene? Why had he spent twenty-four hours in the woods with her?" Finally, to scare Luna even further the prosecutor added, "You, Ms. Fernsby, could be considered an accessory to the crime if Mr. Birdwhistle is proven guilty." That part didn't go as well as Aiden hoped, but Toby was okay with the outcome. Luna held her own.

His uncle lawyer next called some character witnesses from his high school…his coach, a favorite teacher, and a high school friend who all testified of his honesty, work ethic, and integrity. There was really nothing to argue about concerning these facts from his history. The three didn't state that Aiden didn't do it, just that he was not the type of guy who would commit murder. The prosecution was quick to point out that people didn't always know what those closest to them were capable of.

Zori offered to go up on the stand to testify, but Aiden said absolutely no. She knew nothing specific about his involvement in the crime. They had not even met each other until after it took place, she was just trying to support him in any way she could. There was something fragile about her that he could not bear to watch be picked at in front of an audience. Aiden suggested to his uncle that he put Zori's father in front of the firing squad instead.

Marcus MacQuiod was called to the stand mainly to place doubt in Aiden's arrest. To show the jury that there were others close to the mayor who also may have had motives and who fit the profile. Barrister Berrycloth was asking Marcus questions now. "Didn't you have business dealings with Mayor Dankworth? Some gambling? And didn't you two dabbled in the drug trade together?"

The prosecution called for badgering the witness and pointed out that Mr. MacQuiod was not the one on trial. The judge sustained their request. Zori's father probably wondered if his daughter had chosen sides and decided to turn on him for Aiden. He must know that the defense was not fully aware of everything he and Daniel Dankworth were involved in together. Aiden's uncle was reaching to see what he could find out. Interrogating a witness was not a precise science.

"I admit that not all of our businesses together were ones we advertised to the public. We were creative entrepreneurs, but I had no reason to kill the Mayor over any of our joint partnerships. Why would I, our enterprises were doing quite well." Marcus MacQuiod came across a little too cocky. Aiden saw the prosecution making notes during his statement. He was sure the DA would thoroughly investigate MacQuiod's business dealings as soon as this trial was over.

Aiden reached over and straightforwardly spoke to his uncle, "Put me on the stand."

"That doesn't always go well." Toby did not seem so sure it was a good idea.

"The jury doesn't have any real reason to let me go. I want to state my case. I can be believable. Come on, give me a chance."

Toby looked into his nephew's eyes and quietly said, "Know this is against my better judgment, and please remember that you have your fifth amendment rights. You don't have to incriminate yourself in any way." Then turning to the court, he spoke to be heard, "I'd like to call Aiden Birdwhistle to the stand."

Aiden took the hot seat and was sworn in "to tell the truth, the whole truth, and nothing but the truth" minus the "so help me God" part he had always heard in the movies. He felt empowered. It was his turn to tell the world in his own words what really happened, and he did. Over the next twenty minutes with very limited redirection and only a few re-emphasizing questions from his uncle, Aiden shared in graphic detail the full story of what had happened that fateful morning the mayor was murdered. There was a brief moment of silence after he finished while his raw, from-the-heart words sank in. Aiden had no idea if the jury believed his story, but at least it was all off of his chest. He had done what he could do.

The prosecutor did not allow Aiden's euphoric feeling to last long. He obviously hadn't believed Aiden's story or at least didn't want the jury to believe that he had.

"What a lovely fairytale, Mr. Birdwhistle."

"Objection," was swift to fly out of Uncle Toby's mouth.

"Sustained," came from the judge. "The prosecution will keep their comments in line."

"I apologize Your Honor, but let's look a little closer at what we have just heard."

Everything Aiden had shared was dissected. He felt like a frog laying exposed on a table in the science lab. "Describe the CPR measures you tried to perform?" "Why not call 911?" "Tell us again why it took over sixty miles for you to decide to turn around?" "Your vehicle was wrecked and hidden in the woods by accident? Avoiding a dog, you say?" "How convenient for you to follow a dog back to a sanctuary where you could heal since you had a touch of amnesia you said?"

"No not amnesia, but I was confused from the head trauma and all that had happened. You're twisting my words." Maybe it had not been such a good idea to be put on the stand. By the time Aiden's cross-examination was over, and the defense rested their case, Aiden was exhausted. He could feel sweat dripping down his back under the finely cut suit and was pretty sure he had rings under his armpits. He had no idea how the jury would decipher what they just witnessed.

"The court will now take a thirty-minute recess before we hear the closing statements from both sides." The judge gave them all a reprieve.

How could a whole murder trial, which would determine the outcome of the rest of his life, be argued over just a few days' time? In what kind of world could twelve strangers hold a person's fate in their hands? The fairytale that the prosecutor had accused him of was actually a nightmare. Aiden left the stand and walked slowly back to the defense table. The faces of his family and friends looking back at him from the audience reflected concern as well as caring. Toby tried to give him a pep-talk about his battered testimony, but there was a hollowness in his uncle's words. They both knew it could have gone much better. Aiden had gotten rattled up there.

Uncle Toby went to go grab them both a drink during the break and Aiden weary to the bone, rested his head on his hands that were laying on the table in front of him. If all else failed perhaps he could plead insanity. Aiden felt a hand on his back and hoped whoever it was wouldn't feel the wetness there. Expecting to see Zori, Aiden turned around to find the weathered face of William Birdwhistle. What did he see in those familiar eyes? There was love or at least affection, definitely some deep sorrow, but no defeat. His father still had fight shining from his tired eyes.

"You did fine son. It's not so much what happens to man in this life as how he deals with it that makes him a man and you did just fine. Hit things head on." His father's hand moved to cup Aiden's shoulder. "Know that no matter how this trial turns out we're not done until you receive justice." For a man of few words, his dad said all of the right ones.

Toby returned with two Cokes and plopped them down on the table just as the judge called the court back to order. Aiden could use some caffeine about now. His dad headed back to join the rest of the family. The court was back in session. It was time for the closing arguments.

The prosecution offered up its closing argument first, summarizing the evidence as they saw it and explaining why the jury should render a guilty verdict. They pointed out the lack of another suspect despite investigation, how Aiden had the motive, he was at the scene at the time of death, he had the strength to commit the crime, and even left evidence including his fingerprints. It was basically a rehash of their opening statement with an additional slam on the fallacies in Aiden's testimony. He could sense they thought they had put a nail in his coffin.

The defense's rebuttal asked the jurors to ponder, "If Aiden Birdwhistle was indeed the murderer, why would he be careless enough to leave his fingerprints all over the Mayor's office? And where did the crumbs come from? That question has not been fully answered. The prosecution doesn't know who committed the crime. They have not proven beyond doubt Mr. Birdwhistle's guilt, but Mr. Birdwhistle is the closest thing they have so they want to put him behind bars for life or even execute him. Does that seem fair to you? You as the jury should render a not guilty verdict or in the very least consider a guilty verdict on a lesser charge. The defense rests."

"Your Honor, one last response to the defense's statement." The prosecution had the right to the last word. "The crumbs in the Mayor Dankworth's office are irrelevant. Didn't the deceased have the right to one last supper or in this case, breakfast, before his death?" Aiden could see the prosecutor was pleased with himself for his clever play on words. "That's it, Your Honor, the prosecution rests as well."

"Thank you, gentlemen. The jury will now be excused to retire to their chambers and deliberate on all of the evidence in the case that they have just heard. As it is a criminal case, the unanimous agreement of all twelve jurors is required. Due to the sensitive nature of a murder trial and to prevent the tendency to discuss this case with others, the jurors will be sequestered during the deliberation period. If the jury cannot reach a unanimous verdict, a mistrial may be declared."

The trial was over. Aiden's future exited with the assigned twelve. He would not know for somewhere between two hours up to perhaps two months what their decision would be.

Chapter 25 Note: During my research, I discovered that one of the primary reasons today's juries tend to have twelve members on them originated in 725 A.D. from the Welsh King Morgan of Gla-Morgan. King Morgan established jury trials and arrived upon this number for the judge and jury to replicate Jesus and his twelve Apostles. The Supreme Court has ruled that smaller juries can be permitted.

Chapter 26

The 5 most interesting stars: 1) PSR J1841-0500 is a star that likes to take a break every once in a while, it is a pulsar star whose spin causes it to pulse and it disappears occasionally for up to 580 days at a time. 2) The swift J1644+57 star got eaten by a black hole. It was discovered by some of its escaping redirected particles in the form of narrow beams, or jets, of material along magnetic field lines after a black hole one million times larger than our Sun, consumed the star. 3) The PSR J1719-1438 star turned the J1719-1438b star into a diamond by stripping off the outer matter of its companion star and leaving behind only its carbon core. The second star is now classified as a planet. 4) The HD 140283 star also known as the Methuselah star is older than the universe. It is estimated that this star is approximately 14.46 billion years old, whereas the universe is approximately 13.79 billion years. 5) HV 2112 is a star inside of a star. The outside star is a red supergiant whereas the core is formed by a neutron star.

Zori

Aiden's jury had been out for three days. They retired to liberate on Tuesday late afternoon almost evening, and it was now Friday early afternoon. Zori had asked to be notified when they reconvened. She needed to be there to hear the verdict. Her father on the other hand had no desire to step back into a courtroom unless forced. He had been in a terrible mood ever since subpoenaed to testify and informed Zori that she better not have had anything to do with his requested appearance. Her fascination verging on obsession with the accused baffled Marcus MacQuiod and his moral ambiguity horrified Zori. She didn't want to end up like her dad.

Zori arrived early and was already seated in the courtroom. She wanted to get a seat closer to the front than where she had sat during the trial. The jury was not yet seated on the stand. The auburn-haired girl with the engagement ring that Zori had met at the jail was there with a large attentive-looking guy. He must be the one who had put the ring on her finger. The girl named Luna had also testified during the trial and was now holding up a small sign with the words "FREE BIRD*whistle*" on it. The words *free* and *bird* were capitalized, and the *whistle* was written in smaller swirly font. It looked like Luna had taken Zori's semi-joking idea from the jailhouse and given Aiden an official cheering section. The effort was thoughtful, but Zori didn't need a sign drawing attention to herself.

Aiden's parents had not brought a sign with them either, but each emitted an intenseness that spoke for itself. If Zori wasn't so nervous, she would have stopped on her way by to offer her support to his family. She should have done that. Aiden's younger brother waved at her when he noticed her looking their way. How embarrassing. The air was strangling thick as Aiden was led in. He was not dressed in his GQ suit today but in his jailhouse jumpsuit with ankles shackled. That seemed a little excessive. He was not a violent man.

She had planned to bring the murder weapon in her purse just in case it was needed to prove Aiden's innocence. Zori even went to the dealership to collect it and was pretty sure which knife it was, the one with a handle design different from the rest. Then realizing that she wouldn't be able to get it through the metal detectors anyway left it in the drawer. She should have just given it to Aiden's lawyer. Then he could have added it into evidence if it came to that.

The back of Aiden's head was held high with dignity. He knew he was innocent and had nothing to hide. Zori looked down at her hands. They were the ultimate murder weapon. They had welded the knife that did the job. It was curious, each person has a moment when they must decide what to do with their lives. Right now, was becoming that moment for her. If Aiden was convicted what would her life be like? Zori for the most part had given up on the idea of breaking him out of jail or out of prison if he was moved to Starville. There was probably no place on the planet that they would be left alone to find peace even if they did accomplish an escape and run away.

Looking at her cell phone resting in her hands, Zori saw a photo of her mother's young face flash across the screen. She did have this picture of her mom saved in her photo gallery but regardless of that fact seeing the image at this time seemed strange. Zori was not a techy wizard, but she knew she had not accessed the picture. She had however wished for a return call from her mother for years, perhaps her mom was finally returning her call and answering one of the many messages that she had left. But the phone had not rung. Besides Zori knew that would be impossible. Chills shot down her spine and throughout her whole body when she saw a notification for a new text pop up on her phone screen. Even though impossible, Zori could not squelch hope of the possibility. Clicking the appropriate icon, her text page opened. The top name resting just above the list of previously opened texts was the name Vada MacQuiod with a symbol beside it that meant the message had not yet been read. There was a text from her mother?!

Zori knew that it couldn't really be from her mother, could it? Someone must have hacked her mom's old account. But the timing was too impeccably perfect. If her mother was ever going to answer her, right now would be the very best time that she could choose. And if there was even a smidgen of a chance it could be real; Zori was not going to miss it. Her hand trembled as she touched the screen almost reverently to open the view all option so she could read the entire message that had been sent.

Zori, please don't overthink how this message could have happened, just believe. It is from me. I miss you so much and am closer than you know. I'm so sorry for all you have experienced since I went away, but I'm so proud of how well you have handled the happenings in your life. The Mayor dying was not your fault. You did the right thing. Follow your heart. It will always guide you towards "How to Catch - your very own - Star" and never forget, "I'll Love you to the Moon and Back". Always and forever, your Momma V.

Zori savored the timely miracle. How? And why, sizzled in her brain but she wasn't going to overthink it as her mother directed. If she had any doubts where the text originated, the reference to the two children's books that her mother had left for her washed it away. Happiness and sadness coexisted and intermingled inside of her. The word she was searching for was bittersweet. Her feeling was bittersweet. Her mother was still gone, the bitter. But she was here somewhere too, the sweet.

The jury picked this very off-balanced moment to return to the courtroom. The foreman stood up in front of her peers preparing to share the results of their deliberation. Everyone in the room was tense with anticipation. The judge signaled for the foreman to proceed with the decision. A slender elderly woman began to read their prepared statement, "We the jury find Mr. Aiden Birdwhistle…."

It didn't matter what they found him. Zori loved Aiden. She loved him so much she did not want to live without him. She loved him enough that she did not want to be living free while he was incarcerated. She loved him enough to turn herself in and confess her deeds. She could not live with herself if he was convicted of a crime that she committed. It didn't matter the consequences she might face. Perhaps she would get off with a lighter sentence due to self-defense, but she could not trust the courts to do what was right. All she could do was what was right for the man she loved.

Then it hit her. When she confessed, he would hate her. She had let him sit in prison for months knowing he was innocent, and that she had held the key to his freedom the whole time. It didn't matter that she was scared out of her mind or that she never thought he would be convicted. Here they were. Regardless of what happened, even if he hated her forever, she had to do it, because if anything happened to Aiden, she couldn't live with herself anyway.

Jumping to her feet, Zori interrupted the rest of the verdict reading stating her own conclusion, "Your Honor, Aiden Birdwhistle is not guilty."

"Order in the court. I will not condone this outburst." Judge Trousseau tried to silence Zori.

"I have to speak right now." Zori's voice rose.

"And how do you know that he is not guilty Miss MacQuiod?"

"Because… I am." Zori was more surprised that the judge knew her name than by the outbursts that erupted throughout the courtroom.

"Your Honor, this is ridiculous. The girl obviously has some kind of crush or inmate infatuation on the accused," the prosecution added above the din of the hubbub happening all around him.

Zori looked over at Aiden who was shaking his head at her trying to get her to stop as she continued. "I can prove it. I have the murder weapon."

After that admission, the judge had to pound his gavel to get the noise down to a level where he could respond. "Miss

MacQuiod, will you please produce what you believe to be the murder weapon for the court?"

"I wish I could, but I realized that I wouldn't be able to get it past the metal detectors."

"So where is this supposed murder weapon?"

"In the silverware drawer at MacQuiod Motors. I thought no one would notice it there." Laughter joined the cacophony of other noises surrounding her.

"Young lady, are you wasting the valuable time of the court?" The judge asked sternly.

"No, Your Honor, I can tell you exactly what happened if you'll allow me to."

"Your Honor, this is highly irregular. Can we please let the jury finish with their verdict?" The prosecutor requested. Tobias Berrycloth had not said a word. He was not sure where the girl was going, but she may be able to get his client off, something he could not guarantee that he would be able to do on his own.

"Please just a few minutes is all I ask. It really cannot wait." Zori pleaded.

Judge Trousseau was a fair man. He was also now quite curious, and he did not want to convict an innocent man. "I will allow ten minutes for you to tell your story. If not convinced of its truth, I will ask that you sit down and let us proceed."

"Thank you Judge, that is all I ask." Zori looked over at Aiden again as she walked to the front of the courtroom. A swell of love filled her chest for the man seated behind the defense table. She was not sure if his feelings were reciprocal but there were tears in Aiden's eyes.

"The crumbs were mine." Not a great place to start Zori decided too late.

"What?" The prosecution interrupted confused by her statement.

"Please let the girl say what she needs to say without interruption." The judge requested.

"The crumbs on the desk, they were from me. I went to the Mayor's office to bring him some breakfast cupcakes for all he does for the community. It's something I do. It was my bad that I arrived at totally the wrong time. Unfortunately, I overheard a conversation that I was never supposed to hear. That there were some kids in a van out front that were not supposed to be left outside of his office. They'd been captured to traffic; I was soon to figure out. It was a mistake. Me being there was a mistake." Zori started to cry softly at this point, but she needed to get the whole story out.

"It's okay. Please continued." The Judge urged.

"At first he didn't know what to do with me. Then I realized that I would be joining the others in that van. He told me that I was older than *they* usually liked but I was fresh, and *they'd* love my white hair and pale eyes." Zori was sobbing now. No one spoke as she stopped to take a breath. "I didn't want to join the kids in the van. I didn't want to be trafficked or for them to be either. I knew I wouldn't be going home. He said he felt bad for my dad since he'd already lost his wife. I remembered I had a knife in my jacket pocket. I'd brought it to fix the frosting on the cupcakes if any got smeared. I was so upset and furious and scared. I grabbed it, the knife, and started stabbing. Most of the jabs did nothing. It was only a butter knife. I remember he was laughing. I was so enraged. I slammed the knife with all of the effort that I could into the only soft spot I could find. I didn't plan to kill him, just to get away."

Zori couldn't look at anyone now. The whole room knew that she was a murderer. "I let the other kids out of the van before I left."

A stillness settled over the courtroom. The only sounds that could be heard came from a few people quietly weeping punctuated by the sound of reporters rapidly typing on their keyboards the lead headline story that they had just heard.

"Well, that is quite a story Miss MacQuiod." The judge commented, then turning to the prosecutor added, "Could the DA team please follow up on these human trafficking allegations and any other extenuating circumstances surrounding her statements. There is obviously more to this crime than has been uncovered at this time." The prosecutor answered in affirmative, and the judge turned his attention back to Zori looking over his glasses at her sternly.

"Miss MacQuiod, it would have benefitted this investigation immensely if you had come forward much earlier with these claims. However, considering this new information, I think that we no longer need to hear the jury's verdict. I believe all charges against Mr. Birdwhistle will be dismissed. The court will have to look into these new allegations further of course, but I will move for a dismissal. I am afraid there will be legal consequences to your confession, you will be reprimanded accordingly, but it looks like what is needed most at this moment is for someone to give this poor girl a hug." The judge had a soft heart beating underneath his black robe after all.

Surprisingly, Aiden Birdwhistle wanted to be the one to administer the requested hug. Gaining permission to approach the bench he wrapped the broken pile of what was left of Zori in his strong arms.

"So, you don't hate me?" Zori whispered to Aiden through her tear-streaked face.

"How could I ever hate my baking, blue-eyed savior?" Aiden simply replied.

Epilogue

Sunlight City

The florescent green of spring on the mountain has melted into the warmth and color of summertime. High octane tourists who come to bomb down my mountainside on the ski slopes have eased into the mellower nature enthusiasts here to hike and experience the clear mountain lakes surrounded by wildlife. The continuous cycle of the seasons brings new energy and life up here near the sun.

Aiden Birdwhistle has come home. His return puts things back to right in this high elevation world. Each life adds a spark to the area in which it dwells. Aiden not only returned to help his dad reboot their family solar business…it is interesting that these humans feel they can capture the heat of the sun in a box…but he also goes down the mountain regularly to continue studying towards his law degree. Maybe one day he will become a partner in his Uncle Tobias Berrycloth's law firm. They can add Aiden's name to the signage and become...*Berrycloth and Birdwhistle Attorneys at Law*. The name has a charming mountain-friendly ring to it.

Tobias also brings another part-time resident to Sunlight City on a regular basis. He has visitation rights with a darling little Ella who romps through the mountain meadows these days with her newly discovered and immensely improved dad. Fatherhood sits well on him. Maybe one day Mr. Berrycloth will add an adult woman to their team in the form of a Mrs. Berrycloth. Some of the single ladies in the vicinity seem to find Tobias more appealing. A man caring for a dog or child tends to tug on a woman's heartstrings and bring out a delightful tune.

Mom and Dad Birdwhistle's marital issues have subsided for the most part now that their oldest chick is back in the nest. The possibility of life incarcerated or spending the rest of one's days on death row tends to create pressures in even the most stable homes. Healing has also taken place at the high school where some of the students are currently eating crow now that Rocco's big brother has been declared innocent of the crime that they once taunted Rocco about. Rocco seems relieved to have been put on the social map of the school without having to lose a brother to stay there.

Notoriety is only exciting for a short burst of time. Being back to a normal 'Joe' feels just fine to him.

Time will continue to press on here at over six thousand feet in elevation. Citizens will come and go. Babies will be born and old people along with a few of the young will die. Earth will erode. Buildings will crumble and be built. Trees and vegetation will grow, some to be cut down or harvested. It is easy to forget through the difficult times that things will get better or easier again before they return to hard. I have seen much in a century and will continue to see much more. Sunlight City will exist until the end of time. Even if an avalanche, earthquake or other natural disaster destroys the city, it can be rebuilt. And a city is composed of more than mere buildings. It includes the land those structures are built upon along with the area embracing, buffeting, and holding it all together. Part of a city is brought to life by the people who reside inside these buildings, the apartments and homes. Many elements combine to make a city, town, or village what it is. People don't always realize that cities have personalities and spirits of their own. Humans may each help establish and add to whatever they are meant to be, but I will live on long after all of them are long gone. Sunlight City will continue in some fashion and grow as old as the world it dwells upon.

Moonburg

It is time to turn to happier spaces in Moonburg. This story has focused much time at the jailhouse downtown, taken a few stops at the college, as well as visited the Loughty's house and the newspaper office, but let's return to the treehouse. Following a festive wedding party dinner last night at Pax's favorite fusion restaurant in town called *Moon over the Moor* the family is gathering today at Luna's treehouse to celebrate her union with her longtime best friend and fiancé Pax Loughty this day.

A full van load of the Paisley Tumbler family along with her mother Helene tumble out of the rented minivan into the forest clearing. Little Lexi Tumbler dressed in eyelet with a full tulle skirt is going to be Luna's flower girl and her brother Preston adorned in tan shorts and moss green top is carrying the designated rings tied to a mock teabag pillow with cotton string and paper label dangling. Todder Drew is too young to be given an official assignment. There is not a bridesmaid nor a best man present, but the sports photographer from the newspaper is there to capture some candid pictures of the event and a family friend of the Fernsby's is going to perform the simple ceremony.

Luna suggested that they ask Aiden to officiate since his entrance into their lives played a part in pushing them together, but Pax preferred that their ceremony be about them without adding locally famous distractions. Aiden Birdwhistle could definitely suck the center of focus in a different direction and this wasn't a time for competition. So, the professor of religion at the university who worked with Luna's parents was honored to be asked. Her parents wanted to attend in their familial capacity to enhance the enjoyment of their only daughter's wedding, so neither certified as a wedding officiant although they considered doing so.

Since Aiden had become a part of her family, like the little brother she never had, Luna expressed to Pax that she wanted to invite him to either the dinner the night before or to the ceremony. It was Pax's choice. Explaining that Aiden had missed months of any social experience after all. Pax picked the ceremony, not only would he not have to buy the guy dinner but he told his bride to be that Birdwhistle could witness with his own eyes that Luna was officially off the market. Aiden showed up on time giving them both an equally affectionate hug before mentioning that this was the first time he had been back to the treehouse since that fateful day. The forest celebration will hopefully help erase any post-traumatic emotions the location evokes in him.

Their former murder suspect friend arrived bearing a whimsical wedding cake as a gift. His friend Zori who was unable to attend as his plus one had sent her offering of congratulations by way of this edible marvel. The white cake with a tiny hint of green food coloring appeared from Aiden's vehicle on a literal silver platter embellished with green licorice vines swirling around its sides. Both layers were six to eight inches tall with the one of lesser diameter stacked on top of the larger. He shared that Zori had added one of Luna's favorite tea flavors…lemon with a hint of cardamom…to the white batter before baking. The cardamom's complex citrusy, minty, spicy, flavor that was herbal all at the same time, would give the taste a zing and the spice was highly fragrant as well. The unique cake iced with yummy buttercream frosting topped with a mini treehouse made of modeling chocolate then sprinkled with a few living sprigs that Aiden had gathered from the forest floor is the perfect centerpiece for this treehouse wedding.

Luna Fernsby looks like a fairy princess in her gauzy ivory cheesecloth dress and wildflower crown with veil draping behind. Her bodice is fitted with a flowing skirt that catches the breeze as she walks. Small pearls adorn Luna's neck and ears, and white Converse tennis shoes finish off the bridal attire. Pax is dressed in khaki chino slacks with a white cotton button-up shirt and sage green bow tie wrapped around his thick neck. He's not totally clean-shaven but has just enough dark brown stubble to pull off the woodsman groom look. The guy probably would have donned a bigfoot suit if that costume was needed to make this day happen. The bride was beautiful, but Pax was the one beaming.

The rest of the wedding attendants were arraigned in various woodsy colors, tones of brown and green with a splash of yellow here and there. Both mothers had chosen to wear a different shade of green, Dr. Fernsby in an emerald green pants suit and Helene in a grass green matronly polyester dress. Even Sherlock was part of the party sporting a bow tie matching Pax's, the dog having been dubbed his unofficial canine groomsman.

Music filled the clearing from speakers on the treehouse deck. The intended couple made a playlist mix on Pax's phone of several of their favorite songs and his brother-in-law was in charge of making sure they played without a hitch. Leonard Coen's *Hallelujah* and just given way to *What a Man Gotta Do* by the Jonas Brothers. Luna added some string instrumentals to set a more elegant background for the actual ceremony. The couple was having such a magical time mingling with their family members that they seemed to be in no rush for the actual nuptials to begin.

As afternoon drew closer to evening Pax Loughty took Luna Fernsby by the hand and led her to the designated spot under a forest canopy provided by mother nature herself. There the two exchanged tender vows that they had written for one another before the professor pronounced them man and wife sealing their official union with rings and a sacred kiss. There was not a dry eye among the adults. Luna had been wrong. Even her father who had not been asked to walk Luna down the packed dirt and pine needle strewn aisle was touched by the simple ceremony. All three parents gave the newly created couple a hug. The event exemplified the newlywed's casual personalities and planned futures together. Moonburg has been and will continue to be enriched and blessed by the presence of these two elect beings.

Starville

Summertime is gritty in Starville. Residents crawl out of the gutter dripping in sweat to contribute in their own special ways to the flavor of the city. Mayor Dankworth is dead and gone, but another less-than-stellar citizen has taken his place.

Zoriah MacQuiod rests behind bars here for slaying Daniel P. Dankworth. She received a short sentence for involuntary manslaughter since there was not enough evidence to free her on charges of self-defense and a man did admittedly die by her hand. The jury did take mercy on her. They determined that under the circumstances the crime could not be construed as murder in any degree, however, if they convicted her of voluntary manslaughter, she would still spend three to ten years decaying behind Starville's maximum-security walls. Further investigation had uncovered that Zori's claim of the mayor being involved in a sex trafficking cell had been accurate and was validated. The two girls she freed had gone to the police station confirming that their escape had been aided by a white-haired woman. At the time the authorities assumed that the girls had been aided by an elderly female since children's assessment of age is so abstract. The police had been looking in the wrong demographic for the person involved. Upon seeing Zori, the mystery was solved.

So instead of voluntary, a jury of her peers decided to sentence Zori for involuntary manslaughter. They rationalized that there was no way mild Miss Zoriah went to the city offices planning to kill the mayor armed only with cupcakes and a butterknife. She would stay incarcerated for one to two years unless her assistance in calling attention to the trafficking ring could be commuted to fewer days behind bars. Whether she would leave Starville after that time was yet to be seen. She could probably resume her former employment at MacQuiod Motors if she chose to. Perhaps her papa would be behind bars by then and need someone to run the family business while he was away. Many dramas have yet to play out in this city.

Zori does have a regular visitor to help keep her spirits up. Aiden Birdwhistle, a gentleman from up the mountain who forgave her for not sharing her major involvement in the murder much earlier than she did. The boy may not bring as many baked goods to her as she did to him, and those he does bring are garnered from a local confectionery not delivered warm from his own oven, but he shows up bi-weekly to cheer her up and spend time again amid the penal world that he quite recently left behind. Aiden even gathered the supplies needed to bake a wedding cake in the prison's kitchen so Zori could create one for a mutual friend's wedding. Receiving permission for good behavior Zori was supervised closely as she sculpted the masterpiece. The event could even start a new trend…cakes by convicts?

As a former inmate Aiden understands intimately what our Zoriah is experiencing. Who knows what will happen when the girl gets out, but one could imagine worse things than a future shackled to Aiden Birdwhistle. As a student of law, Birdwhistle is working on Zori's case to see if he can help her earn an earlier release on appeal. Although the young boy who ran home has not been located at this time, Aiden was able to meet with the two girls that Zori freed from the van along with their grateful parents who are more than willing to assist in any way they can to lessen Zori's sentence. Stranger things have happened. Public opinion is strongly sympathetic in favor of our murdering heroine. Most citizens do not feel that Miss Zoriah MacQuiod should have been sentenced to any time at all behind bars and that community service would have been punishment enough. We will see.

Zoriah Celeste MacQuiod is the perfect example that an essence of any kind can rise above or sink below the situation from which they are spawned and nurtured. Sometimes with the aid of an added kick in the keister from beyond this realm. Like the fictional character Sydney Carton, anyone can predict a future where sacrifice will allow those *"for which we lay down our life [to be] peaceful, useful, prosperous, and happy"* and that wherever one lives can be restored to peace and order, with a sense of optimism rather than crushing defeat. Every person, place, thing, city, state, and nation has a choice. Each has the right to choose what or who they become…

Author's Notes

The concept and ideas for this novel were percolating in my mind when I decided to revisit Charles Dicken's classic *A Tale of Two Cities* written exactly a century before I was born in 1859. I had already decided that I wanted my imaginary cities or towns to take upon more personalization in this story than London and Paris did in Dicken's masterpiece and for them to become actual characters in their own right. In fact, originally this story was going to be told totally through the eyes of the three cities. It was an over-ambitious undertaking and I ended up mixing in points of view from different characters as well as the cities in *A Tale of Three Cities*. At the same time, it was important for me to pay homage to the powerful main message of the original tale, and I believe it is there at the end of the book if you ponder it...the sacrificing of oneself in the name of love for another condemned soul. Although the love comes from a different angle and my character who looks nothing like the accused is actually guilty, nonetheless, it was a grave sacrifice.

I love names and their meanings. Most of the first or given names of main characters in this story have deeper meanings that reflect who they are. I mentioned Zori's in the story, Zoriah means *star* (from Starville). Then Aiden means *fiery one*. The name originated from the Celtic god of sun and fire, Aodh. Aiden dwells near the sun in Sunlight City as well as carrying much light or fire inside himself. Of course, Luna is the root of *lunar* having to do with the moon (Mooonburg) and Pax means *peace*, he is a peacemaker as well as insecure. The names Vada and Helene evolved from two of my grandmothers…Ada and Helen.

The surnames in this story come from last names that were more common in past centuries which have started to die out in recent years. MyHeritage's blog listed eleven endangered last names with fewer than twenty contemporary bearers possessing them. Ten of the last names for my characters in this book were selected from those names so that they will live on somewhere in an attempt to prevent their ultimate extinction. Endangered names include: Sallow, Fernsby, Villin, Miracle, Dankworth, Relish, MacQuiod, Loughty, Birdwhistle, Berrycloth, and Tumbler. The only one unused is Miracle and I still see miracles around every day wherever I look.

Readers sometimes critique novels for having too short of chapters. Personally, I enjoy short chapters. They keep the story flowing at a quick clip and can add a feeling of urgency. Most of my chapters are close to two thousand words. There is one extremely long chapter in this book (about twice as long as the others) to help give the reader a feeling of time dragging on and on during the trial.

I read the first draft of this story to my husband as he lay very sick with COVID-19 in early 2021. I'm not sure if it gave him any comfort or felt worthwhile enough to share, but it did help pass the distressing time. Hopefully, by the time this book is read by others, the disease will be a distant memory as it will have been corralled and controlled…and the world as a whole suffering from less discord of any kind. May this tale add a spark of light in some small manner to the future and to whoever opens its cover and consumes the contents.

Acknowledgments

Thanks for the request to do a murder mystery, Ryan Buttars. There may not be enough or much mystery, but the suggestion got my creative juices flowing and this is what spilled onto the page. I always appreciate any friends and family who are willing to read a draft along the way and offer input...Stephanie P., Teri S., Julie H., Chelsea and Ryan B., Jill S., and Keegan C....my deepest gratitude. Also, a shout out to Halle Huber my oldest granddaughter who created the whimsical cover for this book. Talent surrounds and lifts me. Lastly, I honor and acknowledge the classic authors who left the world with great literature that inspires us all. We savor Dicken's still timely and memorable opening line from *A Tale of Two Cities*: *"It was the best of times, it was the worst of times, it was the age of wisdom, it was the age of foolishness, it was the epoch of belief, it was the epoch of incredulity, it was the season of Light, it was the season of Darkness, it was the spring of hope, it was the winter of despair, we had everything before us, we had nothing before us, we were all going direct to Heaven, we were all going direct the other way—in short, the period was so far like the present period, that some of its noisiest authorities insisted on its being received, for good or for evil, in the superlative degree of comparison only."*

Discussion Questions

1) Do you believe that a location or place can have a spirit or personality of its own? Do people create the spirit of the place where they live or vice versa?

2) Did you have a favorite city or location in the story? Where would you have chosen to live on the scenic solar loop?

3) Who was your favorite character and why? Were there any characters that you would want to spend time with?

4) Was there a specific scene in the book that you enjoyed or that touched you in some way?

5) When did you know Zori's mother was dead and had not just left her voluntarily? Can you understand Zori's need to believe that Vada was still accessible?

6) Did you know who killed the Mayor before Zori told the reader? Who did you guess might have murdered him?

7) Were you worried about Uncle Toby's legal ineptness? Do you believe that a person can become more reliable if they have enough reason to be?

8) Would you be able to sacrifice yourself for another person if it could mean that you might spend your life behind bars or even face death?

9) Do you think Luna and Pax are a good fit as a couple? Do you think Aiden and Zori will end up together? Do you want them to?

10) When, if ever, did you catch glimpses of Dicken's classic *A Tale of Two Cities*?

Works Cited:

https://www.familytreemagazine.com/premium/unusual-last-names/

https://blog.myheritage.com/2011/04/rare-british-surnames/#:~:text=Birdwhistle

https://en.wikipedia.org/wiki/Moorland

https://www.google.com/search?q=best+cakes+for+a+person+in+jail

https://www.pinterest.com/dimplesjessmez/jail-cake-ideas/

https://livelaughrowe.com/how-to-make-tea-bags-the-easy-way/

https://www.churchofjesuschrist.org/study/scriptures/nt/luke/2

https://www.oxford-royale.com/articles/weird-wonderful-law-cases

https://space-facts.com/the-sun/

https://www.underluckystars.com/blog/top-50-facts-about-the-sun/

https://www.businessinsider.com/moon-facts-2019-1

https://www.indiatoday.in/education-today/gk-current-affairs/story/10-interesting-facts-about-the-moon-1594907-2019-09-03

https://owlcation.com/stem/Most-Amazing-Stars

https://www.campliveoakfl.com/14-fun-facts-stars-get-kids-excited-astronomy/

https://www.justia.com/criminal/procedure/stages-criminal-trial/

https://www.nolo.com/legal-encyclopedia/criminal-trial-procedures-overview-29509.html

https://en.wikipedia.org/wiki/A_Tale_of_Two_Cities

About the Author

Teresa Meyerhoeffer Christensen has experienced all the elements of romance, drama, comedy, intrigue, tragedy, and adventure in over a half-century of earth living. She was born in Idaho to a basketball-playing, college president father, and cheerleader mother, who taught her to love to learn. She married her high school sweetheart, graduated as an RN, survived cancer, raised six amazingly unique children, taught religion classes for many years, was elected to the Bend-Lapine School Board while living in Oregon, and has served on various other boards in many volunteer positions. She now lives at over five thousand feet in Mountain Green where the air, as well as the veil between heaven and earth, are both much thinner and the inspiration plentiful. Teresa finally has the time to put down on page all of the stories that have been roaming around in her head for years. *A Tale of Three Cities* is Teresa's eighth book. Jane Austin, T.S. Elliot, Henry David Thoreau, and Agatha Christie are all distant cousins. William Shakespeare was her twelfth great uncle. Website: www.TeresaMeyerhoefferChristensen.com

www.ingramcontent.com/pod-product-compliance
Lightning Source LLC
Chambersburg PA
CBHW021946170626
46808CB00001B/40